JOHN ROSS

**CALUMET
EDITIONS**

Minneapolis

FIRST EDITION JULY 2025

John Ross. Copyright © 2025 by Gry Lindberg.
All rights reserved.

For information, write to Calumet Editions,
6800 France Avenue South, Suite 370, Edina, MN 55435

10 9 8 7 6 5 4 3 2 1
ISBN: 978-1-962834-46-9

Cover and interior design: Gary Lindberg

JOHN ROSS

GARY LINDBERG

**CALUMET
EDITIONS**

Minneapolis

For my son, Scott Lindberg,
the light and John Ross of my life.

ALSO BY GARY LINDBERG

FICTION

The Shekinah Legacy
Sons of Zadok
The Unspoken
Deeper and Deeper
Ollie's Cloud

NONFICTION

Letters from Elvis
Brando On Elvis
The Roots of Elvis
The Soul of Humanity
Humanity Coming of Age
The Power of Positive Hamdwriting
An Improbable Series of Risky Events

Inspired by a true story
in 1820

CHAPTER 1

The morning arrived like a held breath—sharp and full of quiet promise. A thin veil of mist still clung to the hollows, curling around the heather like a secret, but the rising sun had begun to burn it off, revealing the rugged teeth of Scotland's northeastern coast. Perched on a narrow outcrop above the crashing surf, John Ross crouched barefoot, a silhouette against the boundless sky.

He was twelve, though his eyes might have belonged to someone twice that. Lank curls stirred in the wind. His cheeks were smudged with soot from the old hearth and freckled from exposure. He wore his older brother's patched shirt—never mind he'd never had a brother—and a pair of breeches held up by a bit of sail cord.

Below him, the sea danced in restless motion, shifting shades of jade and pewter. A merchant ship crept along the horizon, its sails taut in the breeze, white and billowing like the wings of a giant seabird. John watched it with the breathless focus of someone who'd rehearsed the moment a hundred times in his mind. He was on its deck, the wind pulling at his clothes, the world unfolding before him. He pictured ports filled with orange trees and salt traders, docks where men spoke in strange tongues and wore silks dyed deeper than the sky. These images were not real, of course, but had been implanted in him by the vivid tales of his seafaring father.

John shifted, tensing against the rock, which dug into the soles of his feet. The skin was cracked, weathered like the cliffs themselves. He didn't mind the discomfort. He liked the sting. It made him feel solid, like something that wouldn't blow away.

Beside him lay the hare—a clean shot through the head. Its fur was still warm, the blood a scarlet smear against the lichen-covered rock. His musket, the family relic, leaned against his side. It was heavy, clumsy, slow to load, but it was his. Or as close to his as anything could be in a life cobbled together from scraps.

The only thing new he owned was the pair of boots slung by the laces around his neck. They bounced against his chest each time he moved. He'd tried them on once, standing in the doorway of the cottage while his mother smiled through a fit of coughing, but they didn't feel like his feet yet. Maybe they never would.

The morning peace broke with a scream from the sky.

John glanced up—too late. An eagle, immense and golden, arrowed toward the hare. With a flash of motion, it struck, talons digging into the gray carcass. John lunged, gripping the hare's hind legs, pulling back with all the strength his wiry frame could barely muster.

Feathers and fur tangled in a furious dance. The bird's wings beat the air with a sound like sails snapping in a storm. Its beak opened in a cry that echoed across the cliffs. For a breathless instant, it seemed both the boy and eagle might lift into the sky.

Then the powerful bird released its hold with a screech of outrage and banked sharply away, rising in a wide spiral toward the inland hills.

John crouched on the rock, hare clutched to his chest. His breath came in fast, uneven gulps. He looked out over the water, but the ship had sailed farther now. It was smaller. Less real. He exhaled, the air tasting of salt and survival.

Far below, on the path that stitched its way through the cliffside gorse, a figure limped—Lewis Ross, the boy's father, hobbling along on one wooden leg and one good one. His back hunched slightly beneath a long, faded coat, and the breeze carried the faint clink of a flask of whisky tucked into his belt. His beard was wild, and his face half-shadowed under the brim of a battered seaman's hat.

Every few steps, Lewis paused as if expecting the ground to fall out from under him. Once, he'd commanded decks and cursed foreign winds. Now, his balance depended on the stubborn memory of a rhythm he could no longer hear.

The eagle flew overhead, silent now, passing the broken slope that led to the Ross cottage—a squat stone dwelling with a peat roof gone mossy. Its single window reflected the early light, and outside, a woman stooped over a washtub—Margaret Ross, thin as a wisp, paler than milk. The wind caught the ends of her scarf and the notes of the tune she tried to hum, "Loch Lommond." Then she coughed, hard and long. She wiped her mouth with the hem of her apron. Her knuckles were blue-veined and cracked.

The eagle arced above her and vanished behind the ridge.

Inside the cottage, everything stood in quiet stillness. A kettle steamed over the low hearth. Dried herbs hung from the beam, their scent faint and bitter. A wooden chair sat near the fire, a shawl folded neatly across its back—the same shawl Margaret had worn when she came down with the illness three years ago. Margaret's gaze returned often to that chair, as though someone else might soon return to fill it.

Back at the cliffs, John adjusted the twine loop that would carry the hare. He scanned the scrub nearby and spotted the ruffling feathers of a grouse. The bird moved warily between the roots of an old hawthorn. Slowly, John reached for his musket. He loaded it with practiced precision. Powder, wad, ball. Ramrod in, ramrod out. Then, he raised the ancient weapon and pressed the stock to his shoulder, sighting down the iron sight.

The shot rang out like a thunderclap. The grouse jerked and dropped.

Across the land, John's father turned his head at the sharp report. At the cottage, Margaret stopped washing. Both she and her husband—without speaking—hoped that John had acquired the evening's supper.

John moved across the grass now, slower, savoring the shape of the morning. With the grouse slung beside the hare, he turned inland toward a stand of hawthorn and rowan trees. There, under a makeshift lean-to of stone and branch, he'd set a trap last night.

He knelt. The wire snare had worked. A red fox lay curled like a sleeping cat, but it wasn't sleeping. The fur gleamed with morning dew, unmarred. Its eyes, half-lidded, reflected the sky as though trying to remember its last freedom.

John murmured a soft word—thanks or apology, it wasn't clear—and untied the carcass. With practiced hands, he bound it beside the others and sat for a moment longer. The world around him felt hushed, caught between days.

With his burden growing, he walked toward the cottage along the winding track that turned up and around the slope. The sunlight poured down thicker now, golden and forgiving. The wind shifted direction, bringing with it the distant, briny tang of the harbor and the faintest scent of baking from a chimney farther down the hill. Somewhere in the distance, a bell rang—single, echoing. A church perhaps. Or just someone calling in their dog.

For a moment, John felt good. And then he heard them.

"Eh, what's that I spy? A fox-furred squire?" Hamish Macrae stepped into view, cocky and lean, with a scar on his lip and a voice soaked in mockery. Behind him, Willy McPhee loomed like a sack of potatoes strung into a shirt, and Rory Bain trailed behind, eyes wide and toothy.

John's jaw tightened. He didn't stop.

Hamish fell in step. "You've had a lucky morning, wee Ross. That's no' always a safe thing, aye?"

John kept walking, but he watched the trail with new intensity.

"That fox'll fetch two shillings if it fetches a penny," Willy added. "You'll be buying whisky for the tavern rats at this rate."

John's grip on the musket shifted.

Hamish chuckled. "C'mon now, we're only askin' for a fair share. A toll, let's say. One hare, one grouse… and them fancy boots."

"Don't even wear 'em," Rory said. "What's the use?"

John took a sudden left, breaking into a run across the heath.

The boys cursed and followed.

The chase slashed through gorse and around twisted bracken. John's bare feet bled on rock and root, but he didn't slow. He ran like the eagle flew—low, cutting, certain.

Ahead, a gap opened in the ridge. It looked wide. Too wide. But he jumped. The wind sucked at him. For a second, he was weightless. Then stone slammed into him and he rolled, the world spinning. His shoulder stung. His ankle twisted. But he was across.

The boys skidded to a stop. Hamish cursed. "He's cracked in the head!"

"We'll go round," Willy panted. "He can't get far."

John climbed, panting, crawling up toward the ridge. But the injury was real now. He limped, dragging the musket. Then, a voice again—too close.

"Ye think you're clever?" Hamish called.

John turned. "You want the hare?" he said, breathless. "Take it."

He threw it high. And the eagle returned. This time, it took the hare clean—and Hamish's arm.

Hamish shrieked. The other boys flailed, falling over one another.

The eagle beat its wings and rose again, prize secured.

John turned to run again, but pain gripped his leg. He stumbled, fell, dragged himself backward against a rock. He lifted the musket.

Willy and Rory closed in. Hamish limped behind, cursing his bleeding wrist.

"You're a right handful, you are," Willy muttered. "No wonder your da turned to drink."

Hamish snorted. "You see his old man lately? Leanin' on his stick like a church gargoyle. Useless and hollow."

John's face darkened.

"Bet he picks coins off the street with that peg leg," Rory giggled.

John moved then, sudden and sharp. The musket cracked into Willy's side. They went down in a tangle, grunting and thrashing.

Then new sounds—wood on stone. A man's breath.

Lewis Ross stood at the rise saying nothing.

Willy staggered back.

Rory followed.

Hamish snarled, "Fool runs in the family," then fled.

John sat up slowly, bleeding from the knee.

His father stepped closer, hand outstretched.

John didn't take it. He stood on his own, gathered the musket and limped away.

Lewis Ross watched him go, then sat on a nearby rock. He reached into his coat and pulled out the flask and drank. Then he looked down at something that caught his attention. John's new boots. Left behind again. Lewis picked up a stone and threw it. The sound echoed.

In the field below, the eagle fed. John watched it, then reached for the musket, the need for revenge surging in him.

He loaded the musket slowly, eyes never leaving the bird, then lifted it to his shoulder. Aimed.

The eagle looked up.

John froze. For a long moment, John and the eagle stared at each other. Then John lowered the musket and turned away.

Some things are just trying to live. And some wounds aren't meant to be passed on.

CHAPTER 2

Margaret Ross had brought the wash in from the line, though her arms trembled with the effort. The linens, wet and smelling faintly of peat smoke and the sea, hung over her forearms like surrendered flags. She let them fall gently into the basket beside the hearth, then eased herself onto the edge of the narrow bed.

A coughing fit took her. It started low, then climbed in sharp, rattling barks that stole her breath and doubled her over. Her hand pressed hard to her chest, and her eyes watered, not just from the cough but from the knowing. There were fewer good days now.

The one-room cottage was humble—a square of stone and timber lashed tight against the North Sea wind. It leaned slightly to the east, as if trying to hear the ocean. The wooden table wobbled on its legs; the iron stove gave off only the faintest warmth. And yet, despite its worn corners and thin walls, the place held the soft weight of care. Of memory. It was a home stitched together not with nails, but with love and stubborn hope.

She stood again, willing strength into her limbs, and moved to the basin for a sip of water. The glass trembled in her hand. Out the window, beyond the patches of tilled soil and the haphazard fence made of driftwood and wire, she saw John approaching with a limp in his step and game over his shoulder. Her son was still a child but walking already like a man who had weathered many things.

Margaret did not want him to see her as she was—ashen, small, fading at the edges. She plumped her hair with slender, blue-veined fingers, wiped her mouth, and reached for the broom. With the practiced grace of performance, she began humming a Scottish tune—"Loch Lommond," she thought—though the melody faltered as her breath caught. Still, she swept with intent, chin high, the broom moving in gentle, sweeping arcs as though she were brushing away not debris but despair.

The door creaked. John stepped in, his musket clinking softly as he leaned it against the wall. He was tired, she could see, and scraped about the knees. But his eyes were alert.

"Oh, what a fine bird," she said brightly, reaching for the grouse with a lightness she didn't feel. "You must've known I was plannin' grouse for supper."

"I heard you mutter it in your sleep last night," John replied, not quite smiling. The sight of her working, though clearly not well, twisted something in his chest.

Margaret took the grouse gently, examining the clean shot. "Through the head. No meat spoiled. That's a marksman's work, that is."

She laid it on the worn tabletop, then turned just as John loosened the fox from his waistband.

"Och! And what a beauty," she said, eyebrows raised. "That'll fetch a bonnie price at the pub. Some grand lady in London'll wear this 'round her neck when she goes to see Mr. Shakespeare's plays."

She draped the fox around her shoulders and did a dainty turn, laughing breathlessly. "How do I look, then? Fit for Piccadilly?"

John grinned despite himself. "Have you been to London, Mum?"

"Oh, aye—long ago. To see your father off, before he became half the man he was then."

Her voice softened. "He was bound for some faraway port. But I remember the theatre best. *King Lear*, it was. So grand. Velvet curtains and candles everywhere. I didn't have a fine fur like this, though."

She brushed the fox's tail gently with her fingertips, then sighed and laid it down. Her steps to the cupboard were slow but sure. She returned with a skinning knife in hand, the light catching the worn edge of the blade.

John, exhausted, flopped onto the cot and leaned back against the wooden headboard, massaging his sore ankle.

"What was it about, that play?" he asked, watching her begin the careful work.

"Oh, it was about a strange man," she said, the knife beginning to part the fur from the flesh. "He wanted to know how much his children loved him."

"How much in what?"

"In money. Down to the gnat's eyelash."

John frowned. "But why would he want to know that?"

Margaret paused, the knife hovering. "Because he didn't feel loved, I suppose."

John watched her stifle a cough and tuck it behind a breath. "Do you feel loved, Mum?"

She looked over, startled by the question. "By you? Och, laddie. If I were King Lear, I'd nae need to ask. You bring in all your earnings. You keep us fed. That's love in my book."

He glanced at his feet, cracked and bare. Margaret's eyes followed. "And Da?" John asked quietly.

Margaret hesitated. "He loves me, in his way. Some folk show their love like sunshine. Others like the tide—quiet, and hard to measure, but constant. He's not always able to earn. But when he can, he's generous. That's why he gave you the boots."

John shifted under the blanket and pulled it over his feet.

Margaret sat on the edge of the bed, the knife resting beside her. "Why don't you wear them, John?"

He didn't answer.

She looked away to spare him embarrassment. "If I had something precious—given to me by someone who had little—I might want to keep it new as long as I could. But better to use, than to lose, my wee, clever bairn."

John nodded almost imperceptibly.

Margaret rose, pressing a hand to her ribs as another cough stirred. "I'll fetch some tea," she said, though there was hardly any left.

"I wish I earned more at the pub," John said suddenly. "We could get you a doctor."

"For me?" she chuckled hoarsely. "For this wee cough?"

"We could go somewhere warm and dry. The doctor at the pub—he said—"

Margaret turned sharply. "What doctor? We cannae afford one, and I don't need one, surely."

John faltered. "I was only talkin' to him. He said the sea air's no good for folk with weak lungs."

She softened, seeing the worry in his eyes. "The only thing bad for me is watchin' my boy work harder than any lad his age should. Now here—"

She held the knife toward him. "You finish the skinning."

John took it and knelt beside the table. Margaret washed her hands at the basin, her back turned, but her reflection in the windowpane looked older than her years.

As John worked, he asked, "How old do you have to be to work on a ship?"

Margaret dried her hands and looked at him sternly. "Put that idea from your head."

"But what if Da doesn't—what if he can't—"

"When your father recovers," she interrupted, voice trembling slightly, "he'll sail again. Fetch a handsome fee, even with one leg and one arm. A good worker, he is. We'll have store-bought food. Maybe even a doctor."

John said nothing. He knew her dreams were stitched from the same thin cloth as the back wall.

He finished the skinning in silence, then placed the fox pelt around her shoulders. She pulled it close and shut her eyes.

For a long moment, they stayed like that—mother and son, surrounded by the scent of sea air and wood smoke and fox fur, suspended between hardship and hope.

The walk into Rockcliffe was long enough for John's feet to pick up a coat of dust, but not long enough to shake off the sting of the morning's taunts. With every step away from home, the dull ache in his shoulders eased a little, though not entirely. Still, the memory of his mother's pale hand pressed against her lips as she tried to catch a cough, traveled with him.

By the time he reached the village, the sun had started dipping behind low clouds. Tealaich's Pub was as it always looked—hunched slightly forward, as though bowing to the sea wind, with one shutter half-hanging and a chimney that smoked like it resented the effort. The windows had gone foggy again, but warm light glowed behind the smudge.

Inside, the heat wrapped around him like a familiar coat. The scent of peat smoke, ale, and dried fish lingered in the air, mingled with the crackle of laughter and the occasional bark of an old dog curled near the hearth.

John made straight for the bar, brushing a fleck of seaweed off the fox pelt tucked under his arm.

Alfie Tearlaich, stout and ruddy, glanced up from the tankards he was drying and smiled wide. "John-boy," he called, "that's you right on time. Got a fresh catch for me, do ye?"

John nodded and laid the fox on the worn countertop.

"Caught him just after dawn, north ridge of the headland," he said, standing a little taller.

Alfie inspected the pelt, nodding appreciatively. "Clean pelt. This'll fetch fine silver from the furrier in Aberdeen."

He reached under the bar, rustled through a pouch, and set out a few coins more than John expected. The boy hesitated, surprised.

"Take it," Alfie said. "Your work's good. And you've a family to feed."

John smiled shyly, pocketed the money, and headed for the broom leaning in its usual corner. Work, then stew. That was the rhythm.

As he began sweeping near the hearth, the warmth of the fire settling into his bones, a voice rose from the back of the room— booming, cheerful, and shot through with salt.

"Ohhhh—you never saw such perfect sailin' weather in all your born days! Not a reef in sight from Skye to Senegal!"

A small cheer went up. Laughter followed. John tilted his head toward the noise, his hands still moving.

At the center table sat a man whose coat had known spray and storm. His beard was a coppery thicket, and his nose showed signs of old brawls and heavy drinking. He slapped a tankard onto the table and stood to toast a grey-bearded gent hunched over his mug.

"To your casket!" he said with a wild grin.

The room went still, unsure.

Then: "May it be carved from a hundred-year oak—which I shall plant tomorrow!"

The tavern erupted. Even Alfie chuckled, wiping a hand over his apron.

John couldn't help but smile. That voice, that laughter—it felt like something he'd heard in dreams of ships with endless sails and skies that never closed in.

The man, now seated again, lifted his mug.

"Name's Finlay McDugall," he declared. "Captain of the Annabelle—the seaworthiest lass ever to split the channel. And I've come seekin' a crew fit for fortune!"

A few heads perked up. Most didn't move.

"I know ye," he went on, gesturing around the room. "Some of ye've had your years at sea. Some've sworn off sailin' for softer beds and duller meals. But hear me now—there's one voyage left that'll make a man rich as a Highland king and twice as remembered."

The hearth fire hissed softly. The broom paused in John's hands.

"South," McDugall said, letting the word stretch. "Farther than ye've been. Past Lisbon, past Madeira, down to the continent they call dark—but I say it's bright. Rich in ivory, spice, and stone that sings in sunlight."

He took another swig, wiped his beard. "My ship's near ready. But I need three good men to round her out. The first to sign on gets full pay—and a half again besides."

Murmurs fluttered, but still, no one stood.

McDugall narrowed his eyes with a grin. "Playin' coy, are ye? Well then—I'll wager this. The next soul to pass through yon door will be so stirred by fate they'll take my offer straight away. And if I'm wrong—Alfie, another round for the house, on me own coin!"

Cheers again, louder this time.

Every gaze turned toward the pub door, anticipation building. But the door didn't budge.

Instead, the quiet scrape of a broom resumed. McDugall's eyes drifted to the side—toward the lad sweeping near the fire, eyes full of too much knowledge for one so young.

The captain blinked, then laughed deep from the belly.

"Well now—seems I've been tricked by fortune herself! The lad's already within!"

The tavern howled with laughter.

"You there, boy—what's your name?" McDugall called.

"Ross, sir. John Ross."

"Well then, Master Ross—are ye bound for Africa?"

John hesitated, his heart thudding like a fish in a barrel. "My da was a sailor once," he said. "Sailed far before... before he came home. If he signed on, would he get the pay and a half?"

McDugall's face softened a notch. "Aye, if he's fit to work."

John nodded. "Then I'll tell him, sir. Right away."

"See that ye do," McDugall said. "And bring him to the Annabelle come mornin'."

As John turned back to sweeping, chest tight with new hope, a wiry man near the captain's elbow—Morag Macree, a lean-faced former deckhand—leaned in close.

"Cap'n," he murmured, voice low. "Ye might not want to pin too much on the boy's da."

McDugall frowned. "Oh aye? Why's that?"

Morag gave a sad shrug. "Lewis Ross was a good seaman once. Fast hands, sure helm. But he's no the man he was. Shark took his leg off Port Elizabeth. Lost an arm some years later—accident, they say. He's been leanin' on the tavern wall more than any mast these days."

The captain looked once more at John, still sweeping, face bright as a boy's can only be when he thinks he's opened a door to salvation.

"Poor lad," McDugall muttered. "Let's hope the tide stays kind." He lifted his mug and drank.

Outside, the wind shifted again. And nobody noticed the smoke curling from the chimney like a signal trying to be read.

CHAPTER 3

John ran the entire way home, the fox skin earnings jangling in his pocket, forgotten.

The sky was the color of hammered pewter, heavy with the threat of evening rain. The wind was up from the west, tearing through the gullies and down toward the sea, lifting the heather in waves and pushing John's hair back from his forehead as if to cool his fevered thinking. His musket, left behind in haste, was not missed. He carried a different kind of weapon now—hope.

The door of the cottage banged open with the force of his arrival. The wind followed him in like an unwelcome guest.

Margaret was startled in her place near the hearth, the mending needle trembling in her fingers. The thread unraveled from the hem of one of Lewis's shirts. It had been clean once, maybe meant for church or court, but it hadn't been worn in months.

"John?" she said, blinking.

He's breathless, his cheeks glowing with cold and purpose. "Mum," he gasped, "Mum—you'll never believe it. I found him."

"Found who, love?"

He held out both hands as if gripping something immense and invisible. "A captain. A real captain. He was at Tearlaich's, bold as brass, offerin' pay and a half for sailors to join a voyage to Africa."

Margaret smiled faintly, but her eyes were tired. "Africa?"

"He's leavin' soon—just days from now! He said he'd take on Da—said so outright—if he showed himself at the docks tomorrow."

At this, Margaret's face faltered.

"And I told him," John rushed on, "I told him Da was the finest seaman in all of Scotland, and he nodded, Mum, he nodded. He said bring him round to meet the Annabelle. He meant it!"

There was silence in the room, but not stillness. The fire crackled, a draft sneaked under the door, and Margaret pressed her hand to her chest—subtly, as if hiding a tremor.

Then she coughed.

It started small. A dry rasp, as it had been for months. But it caught on something deep, and the next cough bent her forward. She brought a cloth to her mouth and turned away.

John froze.

When she finally stopped, her face was white as oat milk. She shook her head once, an apology in the motion. "I'm fine," she said hoarsely. "It's just the wind. It always stirs the lungs this time of year."

John stepped forward. "Mum…" But she was already folding the cloth and tucking it under the edge of the chair.

She didn't want him to see the red.

The door creaked again—this time slower, heavier. The air darkened with the scent of salt, sweat, and stale whisky.

Lewis Ross entered, hunched against the wind, his oilskin coat slung over one shoulder, his wooden leg thumping the floor like a forgotten drumbeat. His beard was damp with fog. He looked older than he did that morning.

He said nothing at first, just hung his coat on the peg and limped toward the fire.

John straightened his spine. "Da."

Lewis grunted.

"I've found a ship."

Lewis glanced up.

"A real voyage. South to Africa."

His father said nothing.

"Captain McDugall's his name. knew the sea like a lover. by the sound of him. He's takin' on new crew. Told me so himself—at the pub. Said pay and a half to the first man that signs on. I told him about you."

Lewis's eyes narrowed. "Told him what, exactly?"

John stepped closer. "That you were once the best helmsman north of Dover. That you could navigate storm by instinct and lash canvas in under a minute. That no squall could twist you off course."

Lewis let out a slow breath through his nose.

"And he believed me," John added. "He said bring you round. Tomorrow."

Silence again. Margaret shifted slightly in her chair as John looked between them.

"Well?" John said. "Isn't that what you've been waiting for?"

Lewis scratched his beard. His voice was low. "You told him all that?"

"Aye."

"But you left out a few bits, didn't ye?"

John's heart kicked.

"You forget to mention the arm I lost to the mainstay chain? Or the leg the shark took off at Port Elizabeth?"

John swallowed. "You could show him you still have fight in you."

"I don't, John," Lewis snapped. "I don't have the fight, or the balance, or the bloody use. And even if I did, no captain worth his salt takes on a cripple for crew."

"You haven't even tried!" John shouted, louder than he meant to.

Margaret's hand trembled again.

Lewis rose a little. "I haven't tried because I know how it ends. I go down to that ship, and they see the peg leg and the slack sleeve and laugh me off the pier."

John's voice cracked. "You think it's easier watchin' Mum cough her lungs out while you sit on a stool and drink your pain down like soup?!"

Lewis flinched.

"You were supposed to be the one to save us!" John cried. "You're the sailor. You're the man of the house. But I'm the one sellin' pelts and carryin' musket loads and draggin' food home with blood on my hands while you sit in the shadows."

"Enough," Margaret whispered.

Neither nale in the house heard her.

John's face was scarlet now. "You've given up! You let the sea take your limbs and now it's taken your spine too!"

Lewis's hand clenched into a fist at his side—but he didn't raise it. Instead, he turned, stumbled toward the door. "I'm not listenin' to this."

"You never listen!" John yelled after him. "You only hear the bottle callin'!"

Margaret coughed again.

The door slammed as Lewis left.

John stood in the middle of the room, his breath coming in ragged bursts. His shoulders shook—but not from cold.

Margaret tried to stand but sagged back down, her head against the armrest.

John rushed to her.

"Mum, I didn't mean—"

"I know," she said faintly.

He knelt beside her. "I only wanted to help. I thought if Da could sail again, we'd have enough for a doctor—maybe even get you to the sun."

Her cold and dry hand found his.

"You've always wanted to save us, John," she said, "but you're still just a boy."

His jaw tightened.

"Sometimes love means lettin' people fall until they reach the bottom. Even your father."

He nodded, but he didn't really understand.

Outside, the sea crashed against the black rocks, and the wind howled with things no boy should have to carry.

The cottage settled into a silence thicker than smoke.

Margaret slept in the old chair, a shawl drawn up to her chin. Her chest rose and fell with shallow effort. The fire had burned low. Only the red-lit hush of coals remained, the glow casting soft, restless shadows along the stone walls.

John moved about quietly, his motions mechanical. He rinsed the basin, stirred the oat tin, checked for any crumb of bread he might've missed. There was none.

His mind was elsewhere. It was still on the doorway where his father disappeared. It was on the clumsy gait, the stiff-backed shame, the way his da had kept his eyes on the floor.

"With what leg, John? With what hand?"

Those words had cut him more deeply than he wanted to admit. Not just because they were true—but because they'd been spoken with something colder than defeat.

Resignation.

He knelt to stoke the coals, feeding them dry twigs he found near the marsh wall. The flames rose only faintly, licking at the air with tired tongues.

"Mum?" he whispered.

She didn't stir.

He watched her a long while. In the flickering red, she looked nearly transparent, like wax held to a lantern.

A sudden thought came uninvited—*I might lose her before summer.*

He turned his face away.

Later that night, John lay on the floor beneath the quilt Margaret had stitched two winters ago when she still had strength in her fingers. The stitches were uneven near the edges. She had grown tired more quickly then, but she refused to leave it unfinished.

Above him, the roof creaked with the wind. The damp was in the air again. It settled into his bones like grief.

Sleep will not come.

His thoughts ran in loops—the pub, McDugall's face, the laughter at his back, the way hope had bloomed like fire in his chest... and the way it had sputtered in the dark, starved of air.

He rolled onto his side.

He hated his father.

No—that's not it. He didn't hate him. He hated what his father had become. He hated that the man who once sailed oceans now flinched at the light. That he wouldn't even try.

John bit his lip until it stung. Then he sat up, knees pulled to his chest.

His eyes fell on the shelf above the hearth where an old, sea-worn chest sat half in shadow. His father never spoke of it. But John remembered seeing him once, years ago, opening it slowly, reverently, and holding a tarnished compass in his hand.

He rose, moved quietly to the hearth, and lifted the lid. Inside he found a coil of thick twine, a flint knife with a bone grip, a crumpled chart inked with distant coastlines and handwritten notations in faded script. Also, a medal—Queen's mark, brass—tucked under a folded kerchief. And there, tucked at the bottom, a water-stained drawing of Margaret, younger, laughing.

John replaced the items gently, closing the lid. And in the dark, he whispered, "If you won't save her, I will."

The next morning broke slow and grey, with a mist that creeped like a thief through the glen and settled over the roof like an extra layer of thatch. It seeped into everything—the folds of wool blankets, the hems of trousers, the hair at the nape of John's neck.

He rose before the gulls started their screaming. The cottage was still and cold. Margaret stirred once in her sleep but did not wake.

He moved quietly, careful not to scrape the floorboards, then ladled water into the kettle, stirred the embers, and laid two thin oatcakes on the griddle. One he had eaten, the other he crumbled into a bowl for his mother when she woke up.

No sign of his da. Not yet.

John slipped out into the wet light of the morning.

The path down to the village was slop. Mud caked his ankles. The salt wind stung his eyes. But there was no hesitation in his stride.

He reached Tearlaich's just as Alfie was unbolting the shutters. The pub looked older in the dawn—its crooked walls and smoke-smudged stonework no longer romantic, just tired. But it still breathed warmth. It still smelled of peat and barley and salt-soaked stories.

"You're early," Alfie muttered, startled by the boy's silhouette.

"Did the captain say where he's staying?" John asked with no preamble.

Alfie scratched his chin. "McDugall? He bunks aboard the Annabelle, I reckon. Tied at the south quay near the rope loft. Ship with the raven pennant."

John nodded. "Cheers." He turned to go.

Alfie stepped forward. "John."

He stopped.

Alfie's voice was quieter now, without its usual bark. "What happened last night?"

John stiffened. "He's not goin'."

A pause.

"I see," Alfie said. "And what about you?"

John turned his head slightly.

Alfie studied the boy's profile—drawn, dark-eyed, but steady. "I knew a lad once," he said softly. "Barely sixteen. Stowed aboard a merchant sloop bound for Gibraltar. Thought the world would fold open like a map. Instead, it swallowed him like a gull's egg."

John didn't flinch. "I'm not him."

Alfie sighs. "No. You're not."

And with that, the boy walked back into the mist.

At the edge of the quay, the Annabelle rested in the harbor like a creature asleep in shallow water. Her hull was dark-stained and lean, her rigging taut, and her prow bore the carved figurehead of a woman whose eyes were blindfolded but whose lips almost smiled.

John stared up at her for a long time.

He counted the steps it would take to cross the dock, where the quartermaster was checking a list. He watched the sailcloth ripple and snap. He tasted the salt and pitch in the air.

Then he turned and slipped away—not yet ready, but no longer afraid.

That evening, the fire crackled once more in the Ross cottage, though there was hardly enough peat left to keep it going through the night. John sat beside his mother, a bowl of broth in his lap. She was awake now, but pale, propped against a pillow with a wool scarf around her throat.

He helped her lift the spoon. She took three sips, then rested.

"I saw the ship," he said softly.

She smiled without turning her head. "Did you, now?"

He nodded. "The Annabelle. She's moored below the rope loft. Black hull. Carved woman on the front."

Margaret murmured. "Justice."

"What?"

"The figurehead," she said, voice papery. "She's blindfolded because justice sees not with eyes, but with memory. Your father told me that once."

John stared at the fire. "He remembers different things now."

Silence settled between them.

She spoke again, even softer. "You'll leave soon, won't you?"

His breath caught.

She smiled gently. "I know the look. Your da had it once, before the shark, before the storms. That look like the world was waiting somewhere just past the edge of the map."

"I'd bring you if I could," John whispered.

"I know, my love."

Outside, the wind howled like something untamed. Inside, mother and son sat together, wrapped in failing warmth. the space between them already shifting like tidewater drawn toward a different shore.

Lewis Ross did not return that night.

The wind built again after dark, driving hard off the sea, rattling shutters and howling through the chimney like a thing lost. John stacked extra rags against the door. He helped his mother to her cot and tucked the blanket to her chin, though her skin felt like pressed linen beneath his hand.

She slept fitfully, murmuring through shallow breaths. Once, she said his name—Johhny-boy—in the same tone she used when he was five and afraid of thunder.

John didn't sleep. He waited beside the fire, every nerve sharpened.

It was near dawn when he heard the stumble outside. A faint thud against the doorframe. Then the creak of the latch.

Lewis entered like a ghost returned too late for absolution. His coat was soaked through, his face ruddy with drink, and the smell that followed him was not just whisky but brine and old blood. His wooden leg knocked against the threshold. He blinked at the dim glow of the hearth.

John didn't rise. "You've been gone all night," he said flatly.

Lewis leaned against the inside wall, dragging the door closed behind him. His eyes were red-rimmed but not furious—only hollow.

"I tried," he murmured.

"Tried what?"

Lewis slid down the wall to sit. The movement was stiff, awkward, almost pathetic.

"I went to the quay," he said, after a long silence. "Stood watchin' that ship for near an hour."

John waited.

"She's a beauty," Lewis added, as if the words themselves might lift some weight from him. "Black hull. Raven flag. I stood there thinkin', maybe... maybe I'd climb aboard and ask for a berth. Maybe they'd see somethin' left in me."

"But you didn't," John said.

Lewis didn't answer.

The room stretched thin with silence. Margaret coughed in her sleep.

Lewis bowed his head. "I couldn't do it. Not with what I am."

John's fists clenched, but he forced them to release. "You still could have tried," he said, softer now.

Lewis's voice broke. "I've already failed you, John. That's enough shame for one lifetime."

John stood. He walked past his father toward the hearth and stared into the dying glow. "You haven't failed," he said at last. "Not yet."

Lewis looked up, confused.

But John didn't explain. He simply turned, crossed the room, and gently lifted the wool blanket over his mother's shoulders.

That afternoon, John walked to the cliff road, past the low stone wall where the thistle grows thick, past the twisted pine that points inland like a crooked finger. From there, the sea stretched unbroken and endless.

In his hand was a packet— a crust of bread, a bone-handled knife, the flint striker, and three coins tied in a cloth.

He stared at the horizon. He could feel it—not the fear, but the pull.

You'll leave soon, won't you?

Yes, Mum.

But not for adventure. For you.

CHAPTER 4

John woke before the gulls cried.

The light outside had not yet gathered properly—only a grey seep through the shutters, like a whisper of morning, not full-throated as usual. The hearth had gone out in the night, and the floorboards were bitter with cold under his bare feet. He moved carefully, trying not to wake his mother, who had finally drifted into sleep after a night of coughing and fever murmurs. Her breath now came shallow—wheezing, but even. A bowl of yesterday's broth still sat untouched beside the cot.

John dressed silently. Shirt, trousers, and the thick wool sweater Mum had knit three years ago when her fingers were still nimble. He slung a tattered satchel over his shoulder and tucked the bone-handled knife inside. Then he opened the door, stepped into the wind, and closed it with a softness that betrayed the tempest in his chest.

The sky was spitting fine rain—needles on his cheeks—and the village was still sleeping under its cloak of sea mist. He kept to the coastal path, boots slipping sometimes on the slick shale, until the harbor came into view below him. There she was—the *Annabelle*—rocking gently in her berth near the south quay, the black hull cutting a silhouette against the still silver water. Her sails were furled, but her masts stood straight as lances, her rigging humming in the wind.

John drew a breath and walked down.

The quay was already stirring by the time he reached it. Two men were coiling ropes on the deck of the *Annabelle*, and a third—tall, with his coat collar turned up—stood inspecting barrels near the hold. This was Captain McDugall, unmistakable even from behind.

John approached with care. His heart thudded with each step, not unlike when he stalked foxes above the headland—except this time he was the prey.

"Captain McDugall," he called, trying to keep his voice steady.

The man turned. His face, red-cheeked and weathered, softened slightly in recognition. "Well now," McDugall said. "If it isn't the lad with fire in his eyes. Come to bring word from your da?"

John took a breath. "No, sir. I've come on my own."

The captain raised an eyebrow.

"My da—he's not fit," John said honestly. "He's... he won't be sailin' again." John hesitated. "But I will. If you'll take me."

McDugall tilted his head. "You?"

"Aye, sir. I can work. I can shoot, trap, patch nets, tie knots—" He stopped himself from sounding desperate, but it was already there, thick in his throat. "You said you needed hands."

McDugall regarded him a long moment, his eyes narrowing just slightly against the light.

"How old are you, lad?"

"Twelve. Almost thirteen. Been workin' at the pub for two years now."

"Too young," McDugall said plainly. "Too small. And no sea legs yet, I'd wager."

"I'm stronger than I look."

"Not strong enough for Cape storms. Or fever. Or thirst. Or pirates, if we're unlucky."

"I don't care," John said. "I'll work harder than anyone."

McDugall studied him. He didn't laugh—didn't mock or send him away outright. That somehow made it worse.

"I admire your spirit, John," the captain said finally. "But this voyage… it's no place for a boy. Maybe next year, if I'm still sailin'."

"There might not be a next year," John said quickly. Too quickly.

McDugall's expression shifted. He saw it then—the fear behind the eyes.

"Is it your mother?" he asked gently.

John nodded, jaw clenched.

"I'm sorry, lad. I truly am."

"You don't understand. I need to earn something. She just needs time. A little money—"

"She needs a doctor," McDugall said quietly. "And what you need is not to die at sea. You need to be here for her."

John turned away before his throat could betray him. "I have to go," he said, voice barely above the wind.

McDugall didn't stop him. "God go with you, John Ross." he said behind him. "Whichever road you choose."

But John didn't look back.

The doctor's house sat just above the square behind a stand of thinning hawthorn and a stone wall speckled with moss. It was neither grand nor poor—just enough to suggest a man who'd made a modest living off births, splinting bones, and winter fevers. A brass plate by the door identified him as Dr. M. Greaves.

John hesitated at the gate, wiping rain from his brow. The mist was beginning to lift now, but the wind still carried a bite. He didn't know what he expected. A miracle, maybe. A word. A tincture that would pull the sickness from his mother's chest like poison from a wound.

He knocked twice.

Footsteps approached—slow, deliberate.

The door opened to reveal a man in shirtsleeves and waistcoat, balding at the crown, spectacles hanging on a silver chain against his chest. He was wiping his hands on a linen cloth.

"Mr. Ross," he said mildly, not surprised. "You're up early."

John swallowed. "I need to speak with you, sir. About my mum."

Dr. Greaves stepped back and opened the door fully. "Come in, then."

The entryway smelled faintly of camphor and boiled herbs. The front room was cluttered but tidy—jars of preserved roots and powders on one shelf, a wooden model of a spine on another. A fire smoldered in a low grate, and beside it, a kettle whistled without urgency.

"Sit," the doctor said, pointing to a narrow bench. "You're mum, she's worsened?"

John nodded. "She's coughing blood," he said bluntly. "And she's sleeping more. Too much."

Greaves nodded, unsurprised. He crossed to the kettle, poured two mugs, and handed one to the boy.

John didn't drink. "Is there something…" he asked, "something you can give her? A tincture or— or maybe some powder for the lungs? Something to clear it."

Greaves studied the boy's face. He didn't rush to answer.

"John," he said carefully, "I've been treating your mother off and on for two years. She's strong, but what she has… it doesn't often turn."

John's jaw stiffened. "So you won't try?"

"I have tried. I've given her every mixture I know, every tonic known from Aberdeen to Cape Town."

"But there's got to be something else—some medicine they have in the cities. Something you could send for."

Greaves took off his spectacles, rubbed them gently. "There are always stories," he said. "But none I'd stake a life on. And none you or I could afford."

"I could pay," John said quickly. "Not now. But I will. I've got a job lined up."

Greaves hesitated. "She's fading," he said at last. "And I know you don't want to hear that, John, but it's true."

The words fell like stones into a still pool. John didn't blink. He looked straight ahead, as if staring at a place just past the doctor's shoulder.

"She just needs rest," Dr. Greaves said. "A doctor in the city might help her."

Greaves opened his mouth. Closed it again. In the end, he only said, "I'm sorry."

John stood.

"Thank you for your time," he said formally, as if reciting something that had been taught to him.

The doctor watched him go but didn't follow.

Outside, the wind had changed again. It blew harder now, colder, and this time it carried the smell of salt and disappointment.

John didn't notice. His mind was already elsewhere.

If no one would help her, he would have to find a way himself.

The cottage was silent when John returned. He opened the door softly, letting the wind close it behind him with a thud.

Mum was still asleep in the chair. Her head had tilted toward her shoulder in the way it did when her neck grew too weak to hold it upright. Her shawl had slipped. One foot, pale and thin, stuck out from beneath the blanket. Her chest rose, barely, then fell.

John watched her for a moment longer than he meant to. He didn't move. He barely breathed. The room smelled of damp wool, peat smoke, and something else now—something faintly metallic, like the edge of rust.

He swallowed and stepped into the room, his boots creaking faintly on the floorboards. He set down his satchel beside the hearth, then bent to relight the coals with the last few slivers of kindling. The fire hissed but didn't protest.

He moved through the house methodically.

He checked the tin of dried oats. Nearly empty. Two onions remained, both softening at the edges. He folded a strip of cloth and placed it beneath his mother's neck, adjusting her gently so her head rested higher. She stirred, coughed once, but did not wake.

Then he knelt beside the chest, the same one he had opened the night before. The one that still smelled of the sea, tangled line, old oil, and smoke.

He opened it again. Inside, he found the same flint knife, the coil of twine, the compass, the stained map. The brass medal still glinted faintly, though the light had dulled.

He took the map and unrolled it carefully. He didn't know what most of it meant—had only a vague sense of scale or navigation— but the name *Delagoa Bay* jumped out at him. His father had mentioned it once in a rare moment of memory, the name spoken as both threat and myth.

John traced the ink line that curved north along the coast, through strange-sounding ports and empty wilds. It felt distant as a fable. But the *Annabelle* would approach it—McDugall had said so.

He set the map aside and began packing the satchel. The twine. The flint. The small bundle of food. A rolled strip of cloth he could use as a sling, if needed. The old field compass. He left the medal behind.

He wasn't doing this for glory.

He rose, tested the satchel's weight on his shoulder, and looked once more around the cottage. The light through the window had turned cold and white. Rain tapped the glass like a cautious visitor.

Margaret stirred in the chair, eyes fluttering partway open.

"John?" she murmured.

"I'm here, Mum."

She smiled. A weak gesture, but it was real. "Dreamed you were already gone."

He moved to her side, knelt, took her hand in his. "I won't be far," he said.

She didn't reply. Her fingers tightened just slightly in his.

Then she drifted again into sleep.

That night, the wind fell still. A hush settled over Rockcliffe— not peace, exactly, but the kind of silence that waits. The tide withdrew far down the strand, dragging seaweed and broken shells behind it like scattered offerings.

John sat by the hearth with his mother's hand in his. Her sleep was deeper now, touched by fever. Her face looked thinner in the firelight, eyes closed like petals pressed too long between pages. He didn't speak. Not even goodbye.

Just after midnight, he rose.

He set a pitcher of water beside her and tucked the blanket higher under her arms. Then he placed a folded scrap of paper on the table near her sewing basket. It wasn't much of a note—he didn't know how to say what he meant. He only wrote:

I'll be back with something. Hold on.

Love,
John

He stepped out into the night.

The sky was moonless but clear, and the stars hung low and sharp over the sea. He moved quickly down the lane, past the blacksmith's, past the chapel where the bell rope swayed in the breeze like a tired pendulum. The path toward the harbor was slick with dew.

When he reached the dockyard, he crouched behind the salt barrels near the quay and waited. The ship sat quiet in her berth, only her lines creaking softly in the stillness. One lantern flickered near the middeck, swinging gently. There was no watchman in sight. He had timed it right.

John slipped barefoot across the planks, moving low. He kept to the shadows of the mooring posts, his satchel pressed close to his chest.

The *Annabelle* loomed larger now. Her hull was taller than he remembered. The rope ladder had been left down. A kindness, or maybe just forgetfulness. Either way, it was a ladder he intended to climb.

He hesitated only once—hand on the lowest rung, breath tight in his chest. Behind him, the village lay sleeping. His mother too.

He could still go back—slip into the house, warm the broth, pretend he had never dreamed beyond the headland.

But he didn't.

Instead, he climbed.

Each rung creaked beneath his weight. At the top, he pulled himself over the gunwale and onto the deck, heart thudding so hard he thought it might be heard.

No one stirred.

He crept along the port side, found the narrow crawl space beneath the forward supply hold, and slipped inside. It smelled of pitch and mildew and oranges not quite rotten. He settled onto a coil of rope, pulled his satchel close, and closed his eyes.

He had no idea what came next. Only that he was on the ship. and that it was leaving soon. And that somehow, on the other side of all this darkness, there might be a cure, or a fortune, or at the very least—*a way back.*

CHAPTER 5

The first hours were almost manageable.

John huddled in the crawlspace beneath the forward supply hold, knees tucked tight against his chest, the ship groaning above him with every lurch and moan. It was dark as pitch, and the smell was worse—mildew, tar, spoiled citrus, and the faint rot of sea cabbage gone to mush. Somewhere near his ear, rats scratched at the grain sacks.

He had brought only what he could carry—the bone-handled knife, a heel of oat bread, a twist of dried fish, and the flint-striker wrapped in a cloth. He rationed the food in tiny bites, but by the second day, the bread was gone, and the fish tasted of bile.

The motion of the ship was nothing like the rhythm of tides he had known on shore. Here, it was constant—both unpredictable and unnatural. A tilt one moment, a heave the next. His stomach churned in protest and then rebelled outright. He vomited into a rag and shoved it into the corner, heart pounding, ears full of blood.

He couldn't tell night from day. Only the scuff of boots overhead, the creak of timber, the occasional bark of orders in voices that blurred together.

Time collapsed.

At some point—maybe on the second or third day, though it could've been the fourth—his throat began to tighten from thirst.

The little water skin he'd carried was empty. He began licking the condensation off the beam above his head, his tongue raw from salt and splinters.

And then came the light.

A sudden wedge of it sliced through the dark, blinding him. A barrel scraped back. A hand reached in.

"Jesus! There's a beast in the hold!"

A second man appeared behind the first. The two faces stared down in disbelief.

John didn't speak. Couldn't. His tongue stuck to the roof of his mouth.

"Boy," the first man said, low and threatening. "What in the name of Neptune are you doing here?"

John tried to answer, but all that came out was a hoarse, croaking sound.

"Get him out of there," one of the men yelled.

Rough hands yanked him from the dark. He tumbled onto the deck like a sack of bones, blinking hard, the daylight tearing into his skull like fire.

He heard boots approaching. The voices parted.

Then another voice—deeper, clipped, and all command. "Is this what we're shipping now? Starved ghosts?"

John blinked up at a tall figure in a black coat, wide-shouldered and sun-darkened, with eyes like hammered iron.

Captain McDugall.

"Didn't I tell you not to follow me, boy?" the captain said.

John tried to push himself upright, but his limbs buckled.

"I had no choice," he whispered.

McDugall crouched beside him. "You had a roof. You had a mother."

"I still do," John rasped. "But not for long."

The crew stood around them in a loose circle now. Most of the men wore expressions that ranged from curious to annoyed. One— an older sailor with a scar across his lip—clicked his tongue. "You want we should toss him back?" he muttered.

"No," McDugall said. "Not yet."

The captain looked down at John. "If you're here, you'll work. You'll eat last. You'll sleep near the bilge. And you'll keep your mouth shut unless spoken to."

John nodded—or tried to. The motion wavered like a leaf in a gale.

"Get him cleaned," McDugall said to the scar-lipped man. "Scrub him if you have to. Then put him under Grimsley. Let's see what he's made of."

McDugall stood, his boots creaking on the planks. "And if he's not made of anything, we'll find out soon enough."

The crew dispersed. Someone hauled John to his feet. The wind stung his face like a switch.

He was still alive. But the sea had only just begun with him.

The man called Grimsley turned out to be built like a tree stump and only slightly more sociable. His face was a thicket of stubble, his eyes pale and unreadable beneath heavy lids, and he walked with the slow assurance of someone who'd seen men die from carelessness.

"Right, then," he muttered as he handed John a bucket and a short-handled brush. "Let's see if your hands work."

The assignment was simple—scrub the quarterdeck, bucket by bucket, from bow to stern. The boards were filthy with salt residue, pigeon droppings, and dried tar. Grimsley didn't offer instruction— just barked when John missed a corner or left streaks.

John worked until his knuckles bled.

The sun beat down. His lips cracked from thirst. A few of the crew passed by and watched in silence. One snickered when John slipped on a patch of fish slime and fell flat.

He got up without complaint, though, which was noticed by some.

After the deck came the bilge—a place so rank it made the hold smell like a bakery. Grimsley handed him a rag and a jar of vinegar and pointed to the ladder.

"Don't drown in the stink," he grunted. "It's not worth the effort."

The bilge water sloshed with every pitch of the ship. Rotting ropes and wet sawdust floated on its surface. Rats moved through the shadows like warnings.

John worked without a word.

Each night he slept curled around his satchel in a coil of spare sailcloth below the lowest bunk, the sea a slow drumbeat beneath him. His fingers ached. His feet blistered. His muscles screamed.

But he didn't quit.

On the fifth day of initiation, McDugall passed by as John was swabbing the middeck after a haul of dried fish. He paused. "Still alive, I see."

"Yes, sir."

McDugall studied him for a moment. Then he looked up— toward the mainmast, where a line had come loose and was whipping in the breeze, snapping dangerously close to the upper rigging.

"Grimsley!" he called. "Get someone up there before we lose that brace."

Grimsley appeared from the aft hatch, wiping his hands. "It'll take half the morning to haul the bosun back down if he goes now."

McDugall grunted. "Then send someone light."

Without hesitation, John dropped his mop and stepped forward.

"I can do it."

The crew went still. Even the wind seemed to pause.

McDugall raised an eyebrow. "Can you now?"

"I climbed cliffs back home. Trees too. I'm sure-footed."

The captain looked him over. "Barefoot?"

"I get better grip that way."

McDugall crossed his arms. "If you fall, it's your own neck. You know we bury at sea."

John nodded and moved to the mast before anyone could change their mind.

The rigging was a forest of ropes and timber. the lines slick. but John's hands found purchase quickly. His feet, callused and curved to grip stone, wrapped easily around the beams. He climbed not like a trained sailor but like a creature that belonged in high places— weight balanced, fingers sure.

Halfway up, the wind caught the loose brace and flung it sideways. John steadied himself, waited, then lunged.

He caught it.

A surprising cheer went up from the deck below.

He tied it off with the quickness of instinct, then began the slow descent. By the time he landed, his breath was ragged and his palms raw—but he was smiling.

Grimsley met him with something that almost resembled respect. "Didn't think you had that in you," he muttered. "Maybe you're not entirely worthless."

John nodded, wiped his hands on his trousers and returned to his mop.

From that day forward, no one called him "the rat" again.

They called him *Spider.*

The storm arrived without ceremony. One moment, the sky was blank and bright, the sails snapping full. The next, the wind collapsed, and a low stillness settled over the sea.

Then the horizon darkened.

Not gray, but something deeper—like burnt iron laced with ink. The crew felt it before they saw it. Boots moved faster. Voices sharpened. Grimsley appeared on deck barking orders that cut through the still air like a whip.

John was coiling line near the forward rail when the first gust struck. It came sideways, wet and furious, sending a wave of spray over the bow. The ship groaned, sails shuddered, and the mast seemed to lean back as if to brace itself.

"All hands aloft!" someone shouted. "Reef the top sails!"

McDugall stormed onto the deck, already soaked to the waist.

"Reef in pairs! Get that mainsheet tight or she'll rip her own spine out!"

John froze—just for a moment—but it was enough for Grimsley to spot him.

"You!" he shouted. "Spider! Get to the mizzen!"

John ran.

The rain came hard now, driving and slanting, turning the deck slick as river stone. Thunder cracked somewhere to the west. The sea rose in sudden swells, heaving the *Annabelle* in wild arcs. John scrambled up the rear rigging, saltwater stinging his eyes, the rope burning his fingers.

He reached the yardarm. The sail was half-loose, flapping like a beast trying to escape. Another sailor clung to the opposite beam, arms around the mast, knuckles white.

"Pull!" the man shouted.

John leaned out, teeth clenched, and grabbed the edge of the canvas. The wind fought him with everything it had. It snapped the cloth back again and again, slapping his face and threatening to yank him free. But he didn't let go.

His feet, slick but sure, braced along the narrow beam. Inch by inch, his fingers locked the sail into its reef line. Somewhere below, a voice cried out in warning. Someone had fallen, or nearly.

He didn't look.

At last, the canvas folded. The rope caught. The sail was secured.

Only then did John realize how high he was. The sea below had turned into a churning slate of whitecaps and shadow. Lightning cracked sideways across the clouds, followed by a boom that shook the mast beneath him.

He grinned. Not out of madness or pride. Out of something deeper—something like awe. *This* was the sea his father had spoken of once, long ago, before the flask and the silence. This was the storm John had run toward without knowing it. Not to escape Rockcliffe—but to become something beyond it.

By the time he climbed down, the worst had passed.

The crew was soaked, bruised, but still standing. Two men nursed sprained limbs. One had a gash across the temple that someone stitched with trembling fingers.

John wiped his hands on the hem of his shirt. They were bleeding, but he didn't care.

Grimsley met him with a nod. "Didn't flinch," he muttered. "More man than a few I've known at twenty."

Even McDugall, crossing from stern to hatch, paused just long enough to glance at him. "You'll earn your keep," he said. "That much is clear." And then he was gone.

John sank down on a coil of rope and stared up at the mast. The wind had softened. The stars began to pierce the veil of cloud. He was exhausted. Sore. Starving. But he had passed through something that would never leave him.

The sea calmed in the days that followed. The sails, once taut and braced against the fury, now hung with lazy grace. The sky turned pale again, soft and wide, and the days took on a golden warmth that seemed to shimmer off the water like oil.

John's bruises faded to dull purple. His palms grew tougher, his grip surer. Grimsley gave fewer orders and more quiet nods. The other men stopped calling him "boy" and started calling him "Spider" to his face.

He had a berth now—not much, just a hammock strung in the corner of the lower deck near the barrels of salt pork—but it was his. His tin cup sat on a nail above his head, dented and patched. His boots stayed under the hammock, though he rarely wore them. He preferred the soles of his feet, thickened and callused like leather.

He had memorized the rhythm of the galley bell, the pitch of the sails, the way McDugall's voice changed depending on the weather. He had learned which barrel held the freshest water and which sailor would trade a strip of beef for a story about wild foxes on the Scottish cliffs.

But he still didn't speak much.

Most nights, he lay in the hammock and stared at the curved beams above him, imagining what he would do when they reached Cape Town. He pictured a doctor's house with wide doors and polished floors where someone would know just what medicine to give his mother. He imagined holding a coin in his hand, dropping it onto a counter, and saying, "This is enough. Now make her well."

He refused to picture her any other way.

On the eighth morning after the storm, McDugall called from the prow, "Land!"

The crew scrambled above deck. John followed, elbowing past crates and ropes until he emerged into the blinding sun.

There—far off but unmistakable—stood the jagged outline of Table Mountain, its flat crest slicing clean against the sky. Below it sprawled a town of white buildings, blue harbors, anchored ships, and streets that shimmered even from a distance.

Cape Town.

John gripped the rail and stared, heart pounding.

This was the place.

He had come farther than most boys would in a lifetime—and not for glory, or coin, or curiosity. He had come for love. For *her*.

Behind him, Grimsley leaned against a coil of rope.

"Don't lose your footing now," he said with a half-grin. "Town's not near as kind as the sea."

John said nothing.

But his eyes didn't blink.

CHAPTER 6

The cottage did not breathe the same way after John left. It creaked more. Held silence longer. The wind sounded different pressing against the boards, as if even the weather knew someone was missing.

The fire burned low most days, not from lack of peat—there was still enough for a week or two—but because Margaret no longer had the strength to coax it into a proper blaze. She didn't rise easily anymore. When she moved, it was with the soft care of someone who knew that even her bones were starting to forget their purpose. She had once been graceful in her movements, but now she drifted—no weight in her step, no fire in her touch.

She called John's name once in her sleep.

The note he'd left her sat folded on the table. She never opened it in front of Lewis.

Lewis came home three nights after John's departure, soaked through and stumbling, his coat half-buttoned, eyes rimmed in red. He kicked the door closed behind him with the flat of his boot and tossed his satchel onto the floor where it slid into the wall.

Margaret watched him from the chair, her hands folded over her stomach. "You were gone too long," she said softly.

He looked at her, his eyes blurry and wet, but not from grief. "He's gone," he said, slurring slightly. "Took himself off to sea like a man. Little thief. Didn't even say a proper goodbye."

"He left a note," Margaret told her husband.

Lewis snorted. "Aye. I'm sure it said he was off to fetch gold and return in glory, like some Highland ballad."

"It said he'd come back," she whispered. "And that we should hold on."

Lewis's mouth twitched. "Hold on to what?"

He looked around at the sagging roof. The rusted lantern hook. The threadbare rug. "This?" he said, louder now. "Hold on to a house that rots when it rains? To a woman who bleeds into her sheets and won't see another summer?"

Margaret didn't flinch. But she looked away.

Lewis stumbled forward, kicking over a stool. "He left you! You think he's going to come riding back with coin and doctor's orders? He's a boy. Just a boy."

"He left because he loves us," she said.

He stopped. The room went still.

And then Margaret coughed—once, then twice. A wet sound, deep and rasping.

Lewis turned away, shaking. "You let him go," he said, his voice barely above a whisper. "You let him run off and chase ghosts."

"I didn't let him do anything," she said. "He made a choice. And so did you."

Lewis didn't reply. He sat on the floor near the hearth and said nothing for a long time.

By morning, Margaret could no longer sit up. Her body folded inward, her skin pale and papery, her voice reduced to breath.

Lewis stayed at her side, silent and hunched. He held her hand through the final hours. She squeezed his hand only once, when the light outside was beginning to fade. Her lips moved but made no sound.

She died that evening just after the stove went out. There was no great moment. No last word or poetic stillness. Only a long, thin sigh—and the cold that came after.

Lewis stayed beside her until the moon rose.

He did not weep. Not yet. Instead, he reached for the kettle, poured water, and stared as it steamed without boiling.

The parish graveyard sat high above the harbor, nestled in a crescent of wind-worn trees and flanked by crooked stones that leaned like old men in thought. A frost had settled that morning—not thick enough for snow, but cold enough to etch the earth with silver veins.

Lewis carried Margaret's wrapped body on a plank cart, his shoulders bowed. No mourners came, save for old Mister Gunn from the smithy and wee Morag Fraser, who brought a posy of yellow gorse and left without saying a word. The minister spoke briefly. His breath rose in clouds, and the verses sounded thinner than they ought to have, the rhythm of ritual dulled by habit.

"She kept this town kind," Mister Gunn murmured after. "'Tis a quiet thing now she's gone."

Lewis said nothing. He knelt alone by the grave long after the others departed, his coat thin against the wind. When he finally rose, he looked smaller somehow—shrunk not by age, but by absence.

The cottage turned to silence in the days that followed. The air hung heavier, as if reluctant to move through rooms that had once smelled of broth and peat and Margaret's lavender tea. Lewis drank most mornings. By evening, he was numb.

Sometimes he imagined John coming back. He'd hear a knock and rise too quickly, only to find it was the wind again, battering the shutters. He'd think of something clever to say and realize he was talking to no one. And when sleep came, it brought only the faces of people long dead—or worse, alive in ways he couldn't reach.

He tried to fix the leak in the roof and fell through the rafter, bruising his shoulder badly. He didn't bother with the doctor. Didn't have coin for it anyway.

One night, shivering under his mother's old blanket, he turned over John's things in the trunk at the foot of the bed—more out of instinct than purpose.

There was the crude carving knife John had sharpened against the shed stone. The bit of red cord he'd once tied around a found feather. A piece of folded paper, scribbled over with strange loops. And something else.

It took Lewis a moment to realize what it was. An old map. A childish rendering, but one he recognized. Delagoa Bay.

He let out a breath and sat back on the floorboards.

That name—he'd told John stories once, before the drink made his tongue sour. Delagoa, where the sea turned warm and the fish leapt silver in the dawn light. Where you could barter a single iron pot for a week's worth of food and never go cold.

"I'd take you there, lad," he'd said back then. "Someday. Someday we'll go."

But he hadn't. He'd gone alone. Woke up three days into port with half a leg and a belly full of shame. And that had been the end of someday.

But the map was here now, which meant John had remembered. Which meant John might be heading there still.

The idea settled in Lewis's mind like a stone dropped into a well—no splash, just a slow, echoing descent.

He sat for a long while on the floor, the crude map spread out in front of him, its folds softened by wear, its lines jagged with a child's careful imagination. The word *Delagoa* had been written in John's hand, bold and uneven, nestled just below a sketched mountain range that had no name.

Lewis traced the lines with a callused finger. He remembered the real Delagoa—the heat of it, the stink of salted fish and rotting cane, the way the tides pulled like hands with too many fingers. He remembered a woman with a coral necklace, and a sailor's knife clattering to a wooden deck slick with blood. That had been his last voyage before the shark. Before Margaret. Before the bottle.

And now his boy was following ghosts.

He stood with difficulty, his leg stiff and aching. The pain was dull today, which almost made it worse—it gave him too much room to think. He poured the last of the bottle into a cracked mug and held it up, inspecting the thin amber line at the bottom.

"To the brave," he muttered.

Then he set it down.

The next morning, Lewis rose with the sun—though he hadn't slept. He shaved. Not clean, but enough to see skin beneath the whiskers. The mirror above the hearth had cracked in the corner. He looked older than he'd expected.

He walked to the smithy at midmorning, not for gossip, but for work. Mr. Gunn squinted at him.

"You lost, Lewis?"

"I need coin."

The blacksmith grunted. "Do you now?"

"I can haul slag. Fix tools. Mend fence posts if ye've any need."

Gunn rubbed his jaw. "That leg of yours not bound for splinters?"

"I'll work from the waist up. That still leaves more man than most."

The smith gave him a half-smile. "You sober?"

Lewis hesitated. "Tryin'."

Gunn jerked his head toward the shed. "There's a scythe needs its neck reset. You do that straight, I'll give you a shilling."

Lewis nodded and limped off without another word. It was the first day in months he hadn't reached for the bottle.

That night, he lit the hearth and sat alone. No Margaret. No John. Just the hiss of peat smoke and the sound of gulls crying over the dark sea. But the map was there—tucked under the lantern, a whisper of something still reachable.

He unfolded it again and stared at the word *Delagoa*, letting it echo through the silence.

He didn't know how. Or when. Or whether the lad was still headed that way. But if there was even a chance...

He owed him that.

He owed them both.

CHAPTER 7

The *Annabelle* creaked in her bones. The old brig had been built for colder waters and quieter voyages, and though she held steady, her sails tugged and snapped with the stubborn tension of a beast nearing rest. For nearly six weeks, she had run the Atlantic southward, her belly heavy with wool and salted fish, and now at last—*now*—there came the scent of soil on the wind.

John Ross stood high in the rigging, toes curled around a wet spar, his callused soles unflinching against the salt-roughened wood. The wind tore through his shirt and pressed it flat to his ribs. Behind him, gulls cried out like children lost at sea. But ahead—there, etched on the horizon like a mirage made solid—rose the flat crown of Table Mountain.

"Cape Town," one of the sailors called from the deck. "That's the flank of Africa, laddie!"

John needed no confirming voice. He could feel the change in the light, the shimmer of heat rising from a continent he had never known but had imagined a thousand ways. It felt close enough to touch. And more than that—it felt like a beginning.

He dropped down the ratlines and landed with a thud on the foredeck. His hands were tar-blackened, his cheeks wind-burned. But he grinned like a boy who had climbed the sky.

"You've taken to this life like you were born with rope in your fists," said Finn McGrady, a red-bearded deckhand with arms like braided cables. "Not bad for a stowaway."

John straightened, trying not to puff up too much. "Wasn't planning to be one forever."

McGrady laughed. "Good. 'Cause there's no future in hidin' in barrels."

They had long since stopped treating him like cargo. It was true, he'd earned his place—mopping decks, fetching lines, even climbing aloft when the older men's knees failed them. And when the storm hit in the South Atlantic, it was John who scrambled up the rigging like a monkey, tying down a loose mainsheet while the sea punched the ship sideways. Afterward, even the cook gave him extra biscuits.

Now, with the promise of landfall, the crew grew strangely quiet. No longer the bawdy chorus of the open sea, they turned inward, polishing boots, coiling ropes, fussing with beards. Men changed when a port drew near—some with dread, others with hope. John, for his part, didn't know what he felt. Only that he couldn't go back.

He moved to the quarterdeck where Captain McDugall stood alone with a spyglass to his eye. The captain didn't smile, but he gave a short nod as John approached. He was a stiff, sun-scoured man with a voice like gravel and eyes that seemed always to measure.

"Land ho," John said.

McDugall lowered the glass. "Aye. You see it first, did you?"

John shrugged. "From the topmast. It's clearer up there."

"You've got the eyes for rigging, I'll grant you that." The captain folded his arms. "But that doesn't make you crew."

"I know."

"Do you?"

John hesitated. "I thought maybe I could stay on—work proper. I've pulled my weight."

"You've done more than most boys your size," McDugall said. "But this ship's bound back for Rockcliffe soon as we unload. I need men headed north, not boys hopping south."

John looked down at his feet. He was barefoot, always had been aboard, and he could feel every knot in the planking beneath him.

"I can't go back."

McDugall studied him. "You running from something?"

"Not from," John said. "To."

That earned a pause.

"You'll need coin," the captain said at last. "And someone to vouch for you."

"I'll find work. Maybe at a tavern. I've done that sort before. You said there were riches here. I need to figure out where they are."

"Aye, and Cape Town's full of lads sayin' the same. Best keep your wits about you, boy."

"I will."

McDugall nodded, just once. "Then welcome to Africa, Mr. Ross."

The docks of Cape Town swelled with life the moment the *Annabelle* moored to the wharf. The gangplank groaned under the boots of sailors eager for solid ground and stronger drink, while dockhands shouted in English, Dutch, and Afrikaans as crates of cargo were swung overboard. There was something chaotic but ordered in it all—like a great animal breathing in rhythm, its lungs full of steam and sweat.

John hesitated before stepping off the ship, his hand lingering on the rope rail. A week ago, they might've thrown him off with a kick for climbing aboard in secret. Now, the dock was his by invitation—his and every soul who'd ever leaped toward a new continent with nothing but nerve in his gut.

The harbor reeked of tar, animal dung, tobacco smoke, and something sweeter—perhaps citrus or cloves. Every smell was unfamiliar but oddly welcome. A horn sounded from the far end of the quay, and somewhere in the hills behind town, a gunshot echoed faintly. The city seemed to crackle with its own electricity, a place of movement, convergence, possibility.

He walked past a boy no older than himself offering roasted yams from a cart, then he passed a Zulu woman with a necklace of bone trinkets who offered him a wink and a knowing smile. A group of Khoisan porters jogged past in perfect rhythm, balancing sacks on their shoulders as if weight were only a rumor.

John turned up a side lane where the cobbles were cracked and a few chickens pecked at puddles. He had just a few pence in his pocket—coins McDugall had slipped him under his bunk the night before. "For bread or beer," the captain had said. "Don't waste it on promises."

Cape Town, in the year 1820, wasn't what John had imagined. It wasn't savage, nor polished. It was a frontier in flux. At the harbor's edge stood smartly dressed Europeans in top hats and vests, shouting about spice shipments and trade weights. But a few streets in, goats grazed in churchyards and women beat laundry against rocks behind their homes.

John's first stop was the nearest tavern that looked like it might welcome both his accent and his empty hands. The sign above the door was a weather-beaten carving of a seabird mid-dive: "The Albatross and Oar."

Inside, the air hung heavy with smoke and citrus peel. A burly man with a trimmed silver beard manned the counter, drying a glass with long-fingered hands. He had the quiet look of a man who'd seen more battles behind the bar than most men had seen at sea.

John cleared his throat and stepped forward. "Sir?"

The man turned. His eyebrows rose. "You're a wee thing. What can I do for you, lad?"

"I'm lookin' for work," John said quickly. "Honest work. I can sweep, mop, serve ale. I've worked taverns before. At Tearlaich's Pub, back home in Rockcliffe."

The barkeep gave him a slow once-over. "Well, I can believe that you're not from these parts, clearly."

"No, sir. Scotland. Ross is my name. John Ross."

The man nodded, not smiling, but not turning him away either. "Name's Mr. Kepler. I run this place with my wife. She's off visiting her sister near Stellenbosch." He paused. "You're not beggin', are you?"

"No, sir. I just came off a ship. *Annabelle*, out of Rockcliffe. Ask anyone aboard—I pulled my weight."

Kepler tapped the bar with his finger. "You got callused hands and tar under your nails. That speaks louder than any letter."

John blinked. "Does that mean—?"

"I could use a boy who knows how to keep his head down and his ears open. You drink?"

"No, sir."

"Even better. The pay's poor, but the bed's dry."

John couldn't believe his luck. "A dry bed sounds like heaven."

Kepler grunted. "Don't go callin' it that after you meet the rats." He handed John a broom. "Start with the sawdust under the hearth. And mind you don't sweep out the drunk in the corner— he's been sleepin' off a Dutch gin headache since yesterday."

John took the broom and got to work, his heart light. The pub might not be fancy, but it was steady work and a place to begin. Somewhere in this town he'd find a way to earn real money—and then send it home. And maybe, just maybe, save his mother.

Later that afternoon, just as the shadows grew long across the floorboards, the door swung open again, and in stepped a young man not much older than John but with the bearing of someone who'd already seen half the world. He wore a loose, sun-faded coat and a traveler's pack over one shoulder. His curls framed a face more curious than stern, and his eyes flicked across the room like a map-reader scanning terrain.

John met his gaze and nodded.

The young man returned the nod and approached the counter. "Afternoon," he said to Mr. Kepler, his voice tinged with something colonial—South African, maybe, but educated. "Room for another?"

Kepler sized him up. "Depends. You cause trouble?"

"Only for people who deserve it."

Kepler chuckled and waved him in.

The stranger dropped his pack and took a seat near the window, peeling off his gloves.

"Name's Nathaniel," he offered without looking up.

"John," said John.

They didn't shake hands, but something passed between them—recognition, perhaps, or the start of it.

CHAPTER 8

It was the cold that stayed with him—not the wind off the harbor or the dampness of the moss-laced stones beneath his boots, but something buried deeper. The cold of the world not wanting him.

Lewis Ross hadn't shaved in days, and his shirt stuck to his back from sweat or seawater or some mix of the two, though he couldn't remember which. His hands, when he looked down, were cracked and mottled, stained with grease and grain sack dust, and his palms carried the smell of rope pitch, though he hadn't hauled a line in years.

His wife was gone. Her voice had been growing fainter since her death, but now there was only silence in the corner of the room where she used to cough into a scrap of cloth that was always just a little too thin. Lewis hadn't been there when she passed. A neighbor had fetched the parson and paid the midwife half a shilling to tend to the body. He had come home to an open window and a sheet drawn over her face.

The whisky had burned going down that night, but it hadn't warmed him.

Now, he sat on a bench just outside the harbor master's office with a tin cup on the ground between his boots. It was bent at the rim and bore a dent on the side where some cruel lad had kicked it last week, yelling something about "Old Sea-Legs the Beggar" as he ran off laughing. Lewis hadn't even gotten up to curse him.

He watched the ships pull in with indifferent rhythm—crews shouting to one another, barrels lowered, sails reefed, canvas folded like clean linens at a wake. He had once moved with that rhythm, a man among men. Once. He had known the names of knots, could smell a squall in the wind, could sing the verses of every bawdy song from Aberdeen to New Orleans. But what did that matter now?

Behind his eyes, every movement ached. His legs—what was left of them—no longer carried the weight of purpose. Just the stump below the knee, leather-cupped and unpolished, scuffed with sand and careless walking. He wore the same coat he had worn the day John was born. Margaret had tried to mend it years ago, and the threads still hung loose where her fingers had begun to fail her.

People passed by him with the same glance—pity, then recoil. Some offered halfpennies, others spit. The baker's apprentice—red-haired, broad-backed—tossed a lump of bread one morning that landed near his feet. Lewis had eaten it without question. He hadn't tasted flour that fresh in a month.

The worst of it, though, was the lad he saw two mornings past.

He'd been limping through the square on crutches made from scavenged barrel wood, weaving between the carts and coal barrels, when he caught the boy out of the corner of his eye. Red hair, sea-blue jacket. A bit thinner than he remembered, but the eyes—the eyes had a light to them, a flicker of something stubborn and good.

"John?" he croaked, voice raw.

The boy turned, startled.

Lewis reached out a hand. "John-boy, is it—?"

The lad's brows knit in confusion. "I'm not your boy," he muttered, and walked off briskly.

Lewis stood frozen, one hand suspended like a fool with a spell on him undone. Then he dropped to his knee, not from grief exactly, but from the unsteady rage that comes when hope is a knife returned too quickly to its sheath.

A nearby cart driver chuckled, spitting tobacco to the side. "Mad drunk thinks every lad's his bairn," he said loud enough for others to hear.

"Maybe he lost 'im down a bottle of whisky," another voice added. Laughter followed.

Lewis knelt there until the cobbles pressed red against his kneecap. When he finally dragged himself upright, the ache in his gut was worse than hunger. It was a wound salted by memory and stitched with shame.

He no longer lived in the cottage. After Margaret passed, there had been no money for the rent. The landlord—a tall man with ink-stained hands and no more warmth in his eyes than a ledger sheet—had come by on the second Friday with two constables and a sharp word.

"Gone is gone, Mr. Ross," the man had said flatly. "I'm sorry for your loss, but sentiment won't keep the roof from leakin'."

Lewis had tried to argue. Not for himself, but for Margaret's memory. She had loved the garden behind the cottage, the patch of mint she kept by the back wall, the way the early light touched the floorboards in the kitchen. But the landlord shook his head, waved toward the constables, and within the hour Lewis's few belongings— his coat, a wooden box of old ship logs, a cracked sextant, a letter never sent for lack of an address—were dumped into the mud behind the stables.

He'd taken to sleeping in the lean-to near the smithy, where the heat from the forge left the ground warm even at night. The blacksmith didn't bother him much, save for the occasional grunt if Lewis got in the way of the morning deliveries. He laid a tarp down over the straw, pulled his coat over his knees, and tried not to dream. When he did, the dreams were always of John standing at the edge of the harbor and pointing to a vessel that never waited long enough for him to catch.

But even the lean-to offered little refuge. Some nights, drunken lads from the tavern would pass by, tossing bottles or half-rotten turnips into the hay.

"Oi, Sea-Ghost—you chartin' stars from your rats' nest?" they'd jeer. Once, they smeared tar on the entryway and left fish guts in his tin cup.

Lewis tried to ignore them. Tried. But there was one night—a cold one, when the moon was sharp as a sickle—when he shouted back. He rose, unsteady, and hurled the cup toward their jeering silhouettes. It clanged off a barrel and rolled into darkness.

"Come say it to my face, ye sons of plague-rats!" he bellowed.

But they ran, laughing. And the silence that followed was worse.

The next morning, Lewis found a dead rat nailed to the wall of the smithy, its paws crossed over its chest like a mockery of a funeral. He didn't cry—not aloud—but tears came anyway, tracing the creases in his weathered cheeks. He sat beside the forge fire, staring into the coals until his vision blurred and his breath came shallow.

Was this what remained? A man of ships reduced to sleeping beside iron horseshoes and jetsam vomited up from the sea?

He thought of Margaret then—not the coughing shell she'd become, but the girl she'd been in Dunbar, barefoot in the shallows, laughing at something he'd said. And he thought of John. Of the lad's fire, his need to believe there was more out there.

John had gone to find it. Alone.

And Lewis… Lewis had let him.

There came a morning when Lewis mistook another boy for John. He'd been down near the quay, nursing the stub of a borrowed cigarette and watching the gulls circle a fishing boat that had just hauled in its nets. The wind was sharp off the water, and his coat did little to hold it at bay. His breath came in shallow bursts as he crouched near a crate trying to remember the last time he'd eaten something more substantial than dried oats and brine.

Then, across the dock, he saw him.

Or thought he did.

The boy was slight, like John had been at twelve. Same uneven gait, same awkward energy in the limbs. His red hair, windblown and coarse, caught the morning sun the way John's had—copper fire in the right light. He moved like John, too. Always a little too quick, as if the world couldn't quite keep up.

Lewis stood too fast and nearly toppled into the crate. His fingers trembled as he steadied himself and called out hoarsely.

"John?"

The boy didn't turn.

"John!" he tried again, louder this time. His voice cracked. The gulls lifted at the sound.

The boy turned, slowly, uncertainly. He was older than John— maybe fifteen—and darker of skin, with wide-set eyes that narrowed in suspicion as Lewis stumbled forward.

"I'm sorry," the boy said warily. "I think you've got the wrong—"

Lewis didn't hear the rest. He'd already stopped, already turned away, the blood draining from his face. His legs buckled slightly, and he leaned hard against the dock rail, gripping the cold iron as though it might keep him from splintering altogether.

"Not John," he whispered. "Not even close."

A couple of dockworkers nearby watched the scene unfold. One nudged the other and muttered something that made them both snort. Lewis could feel their gaze on him like hooks.

"There goes the shipwreck again," one said louder, just to be heard. "Hailin' ghosts now."

Lewis staggered back toward the alley. The boy was already gone.

That night, he drank. Not with the sad familiarity of routine, but with the furious purpose of forgetting.

He stole a bottle from behind the tavern—sweet rum, someone's private stash—and crawled back to the lean-to like a wounded animal. He drank in silence, then in sobs. By the time the moon was overhead, he was shouting at the sky, daring it to split open and swallow him whole.

"You win!" he bellowed. "You bloody win! Take me if you're gonna! I'm already nothin'!"

He pounded his fists into the straw, into the dirt beneath, until his knuckles bled and his arms went limp. Then he wept. Long and ugly and loud.

The forge fire died out sometime before dawn. The world turned to shadow. And for a long while, Lewis lay still.

He didn't sleep. Not really. His eyes stayed open, unfocused, blinking now and again at the dark above him. The cold returned, not just to his fingers and toes, but deeper—in his gut, in the marrow of him. He felt hollowed out, scooped clean of whatever had once made him a man.

The wind clawed harder the next day. It had a cruel edge to it, the kind that sliced between layers and turned old pain into something sharper. Lewis Ross climbed the rise behind the chapel ruins, coat flapping like a torn flag, the ground uneven under his uneven legs. The crutch he'd fashioned from driftwood scraped against stone with every lurching step.

He didn't stop.

He couldn't.

Below him, the town yawned open toward the sea—gray rooftops huddled like gossiping hens, chimneys puffing weakly against the chill. Somewhere down there, men were carrying barrels and nets, women scrubbing steps, children laughing as they darted between stalls. Life carried on as if it didn't know—or didn't care—that Margaret was gone. That John had left.

That Lewis was already half-dead.

When he reached the top of the bluff, he stood still, his breathing ragged. Legs aching. Chest hollowed out like a gutted hull. He looked down at the jagged teeth of stone grinning up at him from the shoreline below, the tide churning white against their base. Gulls screamed overhead, the only voices that ever seemed to answer him these days.

He took the flask from his coat. Not for a drink—there was nothing left. He simply held it. The metal was smooth and familiar. Comforting, in a way. It had been with him longer than anything else now.

He thought about Margaret. About the dampness of her skin in those last weeks. The way her breath wheezed like wind through cracked wood. The way he'd shouted once—God help him, he had shouted—because she wouldn't eat, wouldn't look at him, wouldn't let him carry her to the fire.

He thought about John, his eyes full of anger and hope all tangled together. The last thing John had said was that he needed to do *something*. And he had. He'd left.

"Damn ye, boy," Lewis whispered. "Damn ye for having the strength I've not got."

His voice broke on the wind.

For a moment, he swayed. Just a little. Not enough to fall. But enough to imagine it. Enough to feel what it would be—to give in. No more frostbitten fingers. No more tin-cup pity. No more muttered insults from men who remembered when he'd been more than a beggar with one leg and a ruin of a name.

He edged closer.

From this height, he could almost hear the sea's breath. Calling. Drawing. Promising something like peace. Or at least, an end.

He sat down on the cold grass. Pulled his coat tighter. Set the flask beside him.

For a long time, he just sat there. The wind howled. The gulls circled. And the man who had once danced across the rigging of a brigantine stared into the great unknowable gray.

No one came looking for him.

No one noticed when darkness fell and the bluff vanished into fog.

He did not move.

CHAPTER 9

John woke before first light, the sea air sharp in his lungs even inside the modest storeroom behind the tavern. The rough wool blanket itched against his neck, but the cot—though narrow and slanted—was his. *His*. Not a crew's hammock or a stinking crawlspace in a hold. He blinked at the ceiling, listening to the street beyond the shuttered window—a soft clip of hooves, a rattle of wagon wheels over cobble, a gull's cry that might have come from any coast.

He rose quietly, pulled on his patched shirt and trousers, and pushed open the wooden door.

Cape Town stirred like a lion in the early sun—slow and golden at first, then stretching into noise and heat. John stepped into the street and stood for a moment, blinking at the light that poured down from the eastern sky and washed the edges of Table Mountain in silver. That craggy cliff-face loomed like a fortress above the town, its sheer presence impossible to ignore. Even the clouds seemed to bow before it, spilling over its top like slow-moving smoke, disappearing in the blue.

He wandered down the main track toward the lower market, his coin pouch nearly empty but his senses wide awake. He passed small boys sweeping shopfronts and African women in patterned wraps setting out bread and beadwork for sale. A white-haired soldier—British by his epaulettes—stood leaning against a wooden pillar, smoking a long pipe and watching the town as if it owed him something.

It was not quite what John had imagined.

The stories he'd heard—whispers of wild riches, strange beasts, and native kings who bartered gold for gunpowder—those were nowhere to be seen. Cape Town was, in truth, a port like many others—a smattering of taverns and boarding houses, a proper square with a gallows not far off, and rows of houses built by hands not so different from those back in Rockcliffe. There were no piles of ivory, no caravans of silk. Just the same sweat and trade. Just harder sun and darker skin.

A cart passed, and John stepped aside to let it roll over the uneven stones. A goat tethered to a nearby post bleated once, then resumed chewing on a piece of palm frond. A boy not much older than himself hawked painted calabash bowls from a mat by the gate of the Dutch Reformed Church.

John pressed on. He was not yet ready to return to the tavern, though he knew work would start soon. Instead, he veered off the main road and followed a narrower lane where the smells shifted— spice, dung, roasting meat and sea rot. A wide-faced Malay woman with a bandanna around her hair called out prices in a rapid, Dutch-inflected tongue. He understood little, but she smiled at him with a kindness that needed no translation.

Further along, near a stone cistern, he paused and sat on the rim. Two pigeons pecked around his feet, and the town rose and fell in lazy rhythms. He watched the mix of faces pass—Dutch settlers in tailored coats, Khoekhoe herders driving sheep through alleys, British clerks in lace collars, and Indian porters hauling crates to and from the docks.

It was dazzling, in a way. But it was not magical.

John felt it then—that small clutching in his gut, the place inside that had hoped for something more… well, *extraordinary*. He'd stowed away beneath barrels of gunpowder and bread flour, crossed an ocean, braved a storm—and now, here he was, in a town of sunburnt walls and second chances. Not paradise. Not perdition. Just… life.

He thought of his mother, and then he couldn't stop thinking about her. Her cough. Her hands. The way her eyes closed when he spoke of ships and ports. How she'd smiled, so tired, that last morning.

"I'll send coin back for you," he whispered now, alone beside the cistern. "I'll earn enough. I swear it."

But even as he said the words, they hung in the air like steam off the street—warm, fading, uncertain.

He kicked a stone into the drain and stood.

There was still a day ahead. And a city to conquer.

The tavern was bustling by the time John made it back, the midday warmth bringing in a steady stream of dockworkers, traders and soldiers in need of ale, meat, or shaded quiet. Old Willem grunted a greeting from behind the bar, wiping a mug with the same cloth he'd used for the counter. The man had the thick arms of a cooper and a nose red from years of tasting his own wares, but he gave John a nod of respect and tossed him a broom.

"You're late, laddie," he muttered without looking up. "But the rats'll no' mind. They've had their morning buffet."

John muttered an apology and set to sweeping the far corner. Truth be told, he liked the rhythm of it—scrape and sweep, sweep and turn. The clatter of conversation in a dozen accents filled the low-ceilinged room, a cacophony that masked the occasional shout or slammed mug.

He was just finishing under a bench when he heard the voice. "You've got a sailor's gait, but you move like a thief."

John straightened to see Nathaniel Isaacs leaning against the doorway, arms crossed and an amused look in his dark eyes. His jacket was slightly too fine for the tavern—a deep navy linen with silver buttons—and his boots had not seen a day of dock work in their lives. Yet he carried himself with the casual ease of someone who'd wandered far from home and expected the world to follow.

John gave a cautious grin. "Don't suppose you've been spying on me?"

"Only since yesterday," Nathaniel said, stepping inside. "You've got the look of someone who's run a long way. I notice such things."

John returned to his sweeping, unsure if he was meant to laugh or bristle.

"I'm Nathaniel, in case you had forgotten" the boy offered, glancing around for an empty stool. "Isaacs, if you prefer surnames. Nice to see you again. In case you're wondering, my family came from London, but that was years ago. I've been in Cape Town since I was ten. My uncle's got property near the Company Gardens, but my father prefers the sea." He paused, then added with a touch of pride, "We've interests in ivory, textiles... sometimes expeditions."

John looked up. "Expeditions?"

Nathaniel smiled. "To the interior. Or beyond. Wherever trade and curiosity take us."

John swallowed and leaned the broom against the wall. "Sounds grand."

"It has its dull bits," Nathaniel said, waving to Old Willem for something cool to drink. "Endless negotiations. Sore feet. Dust in every crevice. But there are moments... I've met Zulu traders who carry spears older than your kingdom. Seen elephants pass so close they shook the earth like thunder."

He said it lightly, but the words lit a spark in John's chest. This was what he'd pictured. *This*—something more than fishmongers and coopers, something larger than soot and ships.

Nathaniel caught his expression. "And you?"

"Scotland," John said. "Just arrived. My ship's headed back without me."

"A stowaway, then," Nathaniel said with a raised brow.

John flushed but didn't deny it.

"Brave or foolish," Nathaniel said, then nodded as if it were both. "Either way, you're here now. What's the plan?"

John hesitated. He hadn't said it aloud before. "Work. Save money. Send for my mum."

Nathaniel's brow creased, just faintly. "She's back in Scotland?"

John nodded. "Aye. Sick."

Nathaniel looked down, his fingers tracing the rim of the mug that had appeared before him. "Then I hope Cape Town's kind to you," he said at last. "It can be, when it wants to be."

John looked at him then—not at his fine coat or polished boots, but at the way he sat, easy but alert, with eyes that had seen more than his years. He was a boy of the world, no doubt. But not untouched by pain. Not immune to loss.

"Maybe," John said, "we'll both get what we came for."

Nathaniel raised his mug in salute. "Or something better."

Cape Town, when seen from the deck of a ship at sunrise, had shimmered like something out of a painted dream—whitewashed walls gleaming beneath the sloping green of Table Mountain, a crescent of roofs along the bay like a welcoming arm. But with his boots now on the earth, John discovered something different.

The air still smelled of salt and spice, yes, but it was mingled with the reek of dung and sweat and the offal of butcher stalls. The alleys behind the warehouses stank, and the mud never quite dried, no matter how fierce the sun. Ragged dogs wandered at will, and not all the faces on the street were friendly ones.

Nathaniel walked beside him, narrating with the pride of a local guide.

"That's the Dutch Reformed Church," he said, pointing at a stone structure with broad steps and shuttered windows. "The bells are iron, cast in Amsterdam. And over there, that's the Castle of Good Hope. The oldest colonial building in the whole region. The garrison drills in the square every Thursday."

John followed his gestures, but his face was less impressed than puzzled. "It's just a fort," he muttered. "An' that's just a kirk. I've seen finer."

Nathaniel chuckled. "Aye, but you've come too full of fire. You expected jewels in the gutters, didn't you?"

"I expected…" John faltered. "Something different. Bigger. Wilder."

"Oh, it's wild," Nathaniel said, slowing his steps. "But it hides its teeth during the day."

They passed Malay women in bright scarves selling cakes from shallow trays, and a British soldier arguing with a man over a spilled sack of peppercorns. In the narrow quarter near the slave lodge, John saw men in iron collars doing quiet labor under the eyes of armed overseers.

He turned to Nathaniel with a frown. "I thought the slave trade was ended."

Nathaniel's voice dropped. "Officially. But it takes longer for law to touch every hand. Some say the shackles just changed shape."

They rounded a corner and entered the edge of the Company Gardens, where dusty palms lined the path and a shallow canal ran with water cold and clear from the mountain. Children chased ducks, and a British family picnicked under a camphor tree. The air here was gentler. Civilized.

John sat on a low stone wall and stared across the grounds. "There's no magic here," he said softly. "No adventure. Just folk living and trying not to starve."

Nathaniel joined him, brushing dust from his trousers. "And yet—here we are. You and I. From different corners of the world, sharing bread under a palm tree at the foot of a mountain."

John gave a short laugh. "It's not bread."

"No," Nathaniel agreed, pulling out a small twist of biltong. "But it'll do for lunch."

They chewed in silence for a while.

"You ever feel like you came too late?" John asked. "Like all the great voyages have already been sailed? That the world's been found already?"

Nathaniel tilted his head. "Then maybe we have to lose it again. Unlearn what the maps say. Find the edges no one else dares walk."

John looked at him, uncertain whether the words were foolish or brilliant. But they warmed something in his gut, something that reminded him of stories whispered by candlelight, of the smell of old parchment, of stars reflected in black water.

He stood up suddenly. "Come on."

"Where?"

"Back to the tavern. I've a floor to scrub, and you've tales yet to earn."

Nathaniel followed, grinning. "Aye, captain."

The quarrel began with a shove. Just one—a careless bump of shoulders between a boy barely taller than a rain barrel and two older lads who had claimed a patch of alley behind the fishmonger's stall as their kingdom.

The smaller boy, barefoot and tattered like John back in Scotland, had only been trying to cut through with a parcel of bread, likely on errand for some kitchen. One of the older boys knocked the loaf to the dirt, then laughed as he stepped on it. "Think we'll let ye pass, ratling?"

The little one tried to back away, but another grabbed his collar.

John saw it from across the square. He had been helping shift a cartload of melons for the tavernkeeper when the commotion drew his eyes. He dropped the burlap sack without a word and moved across the street, his jaw already tight.

"Oi!" John barked. "Pick on someone who'll hit back."

The two bullies turned, staring like mad dogs. "You that new lad from the port tavern?" one jeered. "Think you've the right to boss about in Cape Town, do ye?"

John didn't answer. He stepped between them and the trembling boy, who clutched the ruined loaf like a shield.

"You've made your joke. That's enough."

The taller bully shoved John hard. John stumbled but didn't fall. Instead, he ducked low and surged upward like he'd done swinging to the cross-spar in the Annabelle's rigging. His shoulder caught the boy in the chest, and the two of them went down in a tangle.

The other came at him with fists, but John twisted, landing a sharp elbow into the side of the boy's neck. It wasn't elegant, but it worked. The first got up bleeding from the lip and backed off, flinging such obscenities that some local women covered their children's ears. The second boy scrambled to his feet and followed, one eye already swelling.

The whole thing was over in seconds.

"Ye all right?" John asked the small boy, who nodded mutely and clutched his parcel tighter.

The boy nodded.

John helped him brush off the dirt and pointed him in the direction of the kitchens. "Off ye go now."

From a shaded post nearby, Nathaniel Isaacs had been watching. He said nothing until John turned back across the square. "That was poorly done," Nathaniel remarked as John approached.

John's shoulders straightened. "He was smaller than them. They crushed his bread."

Nathaniel nodded slowly. "Still. You'll bruise your knuckles before you make a dent in this town's cruelty."

John shook his hand once, blood darkening a split in his palm. "Maybe. But I'd rather bruise them than keep still."

Nathaniel studied him. "How old are you?"

"Twelve."

"And you crossed the sea alone?"

John's chin lifted. "Aye. Stowed away on the Annabelle. Earned my keep by the ropes."

"You've the look of one born to the mast." Nathaniel folded his arms, then added more softly, "Not many lads your age would take a blow for a stranger."

John shrugged. "I don't much care for bullies."

Nathaniel smiled, the first real smile John had seen from him. "Nor do I." He was quiet for a moment, then said, "There's something brewing. A voyage. Dangerous, but promising. I'm not the one to decide who joins it—but I'll tell you this. Men who stand for the smaller ones tend to go far, even when the map ends."

John's brow furrowed. "What kind of voyage?"

Nathaniel didn't answer. Instead, he gave a slight nod. "If you've any interest in such things, you'd do well to keep close."

And with that, he stepped back into the crowd, leaving John alone beside the square, his bloodied hand and swelling pride balanced between fear and fascination.

He didn't know it yet, but something had shifted.

Not just in how Nathaniel saw him—but in the shape of the road ahead.

CHAPTER 10

He had come to the cliff before, more times than he cared to count. Sometimes drunk, sometimes weeping, sometimes half-convinced the wind itself was trying to talk him into jumping. But Lewis had never gone farther than the edge.

This morning was colder than it should've been. A hard, pitiless cold, the kind that settled in your bones and made even breath feel like judgment. The sea below clawed at the rocks, not with rage but persistence—a sound Lewis had come to recognize in himself.

He stood at the cliff's lip, coat unbuttoned, hands hanging limp. His beard had grown wild and matted in places, and his face—once the kind that turned heads on a wharf—was now pitted, drawn, and lined by ruin. He hadn't spoken to another soul in two days, unless you counted his bitter arguments with Margaret's ghost.

A gull darted overhead. He didn't look up.

He'd dreamt last night that Margaret was still in the bed, just thin and quiet and breathing in her old way. She'd asked him what he'd done with her wedding ring. He'd had no answer, because in waking life he'd sold it for whisky.

And John... John had gone off to God-knows-where. Maybe the lad hated him now. Maybe he should. Maybe it was better if the boy never came back.

The thought hit him hard. He swayed slightly forward.

But then—just as the thought turned black and full of gravity—he caught something. A shimmer.

There, far out on the horizon, where the sky met the sea like old pages stitched shut, a sail. Just one, ivory white, billowed out like a lung full of purpose. The ship cut clean against the wind, its motion slow but sure, a certainty stitched into water.

Lewis narrowed his eyes. Something tightened in his chest.

He'd once lived for that motion. For the rigging's snap, the salt on his face, the promise of another coast. He'd told stories of Delagoa Bay, of lanterns flickering in monsoon dusk, of narrow escapes and markets heavy with spice. John had listened once. Eyes wide. Heart open.

John clenched his fists now, not to jump but to feel the blood return to his fingers. "Maybe you're out there, boy," he muttered. "Maybe you're out there lookin' for more than this cursed place."

He stepped back from the edge. Just one step. But it was enough. The cold stayed. It always did. But now, it wasn't the only thing left in him.

He walked back down the slope like a man waking from a half-remembered sleep. The town below hadn't changed. Still gray, still wet, still half-bent with the weight of its own hopelessness. But Lewis felt the walk differently this time. His legs burned, the muscles clumsy from too many months of sag and stumble. His chest ached with the climb, his breath sharp in his throat. But he welcomed it.

A boy threw a stone from the side alley of the tannery, missing Lewis by feet but laughing anyway. Lewis didn't shout this time. Didn't glare. Just kept walking.

At the pump, he cupped water into his beard and rinsed the salt from his cheeks. Some of the old women still muttered when they passed him. He was used to that. But one or two looked confused now, like they weren't sure if they recognized him, or if the man they thought they saw had crawled out of a memory.

He made it back to the old cottage not rented since he was booted out and stood in the doorway for a long time. The fire had gone out. The shutters hung crooked on one hinge. Margaret's scarf was still pinned above the hearth where she used to hang it to dry. His eyes caught on it.

"Still here," he said aloud. "So am I."

He cleared the corner of the floor where the bottles had gathered and stacked them by the door, one by one. He found the brush John used to use and dragged it along the hearthstones, scrubbing soot that had no reason to be cleaned except that it was filth. It felt strange to care. But he did.

Later, when the light dipped low, he lit a single candle and sat with his back against the far wall, legs out, arms folded. He stared at the flame and tried to remember the last time he'd held a rope in his hands. A sail. A compass.

He could feel his arms again. Not just as tools of grief or fists of rage—but as his own.

He didn't say it out loud, not yet, but a thought had begun to form. If John had truly gone to sea, Lewis would find him. Not tomorrow. Maybe not even soon. But someday.

He would not let Margaret be the last good thing he'd loved.

Lewis stayed in the ramshackle outbuilding the blacksmith had once used for storing bent nails and broken tack, a low squat structure that leaned like a drunkard into the wind. It was hardly fit for a man to live in, but no one had the heart—or perhaps the cruelty—to force him back onto the road. The blacksmith's wife, a square-jawed woman with salt-gray hair pulled into a tight coil, left him scraps sometimes—heel ends of bread, broth with too much salt. They said little to each other. But in this small act of routine mercy, Lewis clung to a shadow of belonging.

That evening, he shuffled back under the dimming sky, the clang of the blacksmith's hammer echoing like some grim church bell tolling him to judgment. He passed the main house quietly, shoulders stooped. A child in the doorway stared at him without fear or pity. Just stared. Lewis had grown used to those looks.

Inside the outbuilding, the air smelled of rust and old soot. He lit a stub of tallow candle and sank onto the bundle of hay he called a bed. His shoulder ached—the cold always found its way in—and he rubbed it absently while his thoughts churned like wind-waves on the firth.

He reached for the letter again. It was not John's handwriting, not yet. But he was certain his son would write when he had something to write about. He had to. Lewis unfolded the parchment as if it might give off warmth, staring at the words he could now recite by heart. He had lifted it a while back from a shop stall, not proud of stealing it, not ashamed either. It was simply a shipping notice from Cape Town—a port of promise. He had pretended, for a moment, that it had come from John—had even made up the text of his son's message: "I'm well, Da. I've found work with a proper ship and will soon earn enough to send for you and Mum. Don't give up."

But in reality there was no such letter. Only the hope of one. And now, no Margaret. No John. Only that distant wind and the groaning timbers of a building meant for broken tools.

He lay back, folding the letter to his chest. In the quiet, he felt the weight of every bruise that life had dealt him, and the bitter ache of those he'd dealt himself.

Outside, the hammering stopped—a merciful pause in the world. Then came the howl of a dog or a child—Lewis couldn't tell. It cut through the night like some grim herald. He pulled the blanket tighter over himself, willing the world to forget him.

But part of him stirred. Just not enough to rise. Not yet.

He hadn't spoken to a ship's man in years. Even while passing the docks, Lewis had kept his eyes down, skirting the edge of the quays like a dog afraid of the boot. But now, drawn by the scent of tar and salt, he found himself pausing beneath the rigging of a coastal lugger, watching the crew haul sacks ashore with methodical grunts. Their shirts clung to sweat-darkened backs, arms corded with labor.

He knew that labor. His body remembered.

He approached a tall lad sorting line near the gangplank. "Where'd she come from?" Lewis asked, voice gruff from disuse.

The lad looked up. "Kirkcaldy. Took on kelp and stone. Back again in five days."

Lewis nodded, then moved on before the boy could ask anything in return. He didn't want questions. Not yet.

Over the next week, he lingered more. Watched the coming and going of vessels—trading boats, mail runners, fishing sloops. He began to ask names. Not of men, but of ships. Routes. Timelines. He learned which boats headed down-coast toward England, which cut west toward Ireland, and which, more rarely, turned south toward the continent—or beyond.

One afternoon, huddled near the warehouse ledgers posted behind glass, he saw the name *Annabelle*. The ink was dated weeks past.

Destination: Cape Town.

His pulse thudded.

It had to be the same ship. The one the boy had spoken of. The one that had docked once before, recruiting.

He didn't know for certain that John had gone aboard. But the fire in his gut said he had—said that the boy, wild as he was, would've done anything to spare his mother. Even run.

And if he had...

Lewis turned from the ledger and walked toward the sea. He stood at the cliff again, but this time, the wind seemed warmer. Braver. The sails out on the horizon curled like wings, white and full.

He did not weep. But his jaw trembled.

That night, he sat by the fire and drafted a list. Just a few items. But the act steadied his hand. Rope. Knife. Canteen. Journal. He would need to recover these things slowly, without drawing attention.

He had no money. But he had time. And for the first time in years, he had a purpose.

The next morning, he shaved his beard. The man in the cracked mirror was older, yes—but his eyes had cleared. They were not the eyes of a ghost.

They were the eyes of a father looking for his son.

CHAPTER 11

It had been several weeks since John had first met Nathaniel Isaacs on the wooden stoop of the tavern. The days that followed had not been uneventful. Cape Town, though modest in size and colonial in its manners, pulsed with the tide of the sea—ships came and went, bringing sailors, rumors, and the occasional barrel of Portuguese wine. And as the city bustled, so too did John's days spent sweeping floors, hauling crates, and minding the whims of patrons who cared little for the efforts of a boy without coin or name.

But not Nathaniel.

Since that first day, something in John had stirred the older boy's interest. Perhaps it was the way John held himself—upright and direct, unbowed by hardship. Or perhaps it was that Nathaniel saw in John the ghost of his own younger brother, Levi, who had died of a fever in London some four years before. Whatever the reason, the two had grown close, though neither would have called it friendship aloud. Friendship, after all, was something boys admitted to when no one else could hear.

They spent stolen hours by the harbor, watching the ships bob and strain against their moorings. Nathaniel, full of knowledge passed down from his father's ledgers and his uncle's letters, would name them all—barques, brigs, schooners. John, always the listener, would ask questions—about faraway ports, about the languages spoken along the coasts of India, or what kind of beast left tusks taller than a man on the shores of Mozambique.

"There's talk," Nathaniel said one afternoon as they sat on overturned barrels, munching on stale biscuits from the dockmaster's pantry, "of outfitting a new expedition north. Beyond Port Elizabeth. Into Natal."

John looked up from his crumbs. "Who's talking?"

"My uncle. Saul Solomon the elder. A proper merchant, loud of voice and tight of purse." Nathaniel smirked. "But generous when his name's attached to something daring. Seems there's worry over a party gone missing."

John frowned. "Dead?"

"Maybe. Or just too far gone to be found by letter."

Nathaniel spoke with the careless confidence of someone accustomed to watching others solve problems. John, by contrast, bore the look of someone who had lived as the problem to be solved. But something in this news tugged at him—a whisper of purpose, a thrill that sounded like a calling.

"They'll need men," Nathaniel continued. "Or boys, in our case."

John leaned forward. "You mean to go?"

"If my uncle will have me. He's agreed to fund part of the mission. Lieutenant King of the *Mary* will captain the brig. Once she's done discharging cargo, she'll set sail."

"And you'll be crew?"

Nathaniel smiled crookedly. "Hardly. I'm to be King's 'companion.' It's a useless title, really. But it gets me aboard."

"What about me?"

Nathaniel gave him a long look, weighing something invisible.

"You," he said slowly, "might be harder to justify. No letters no education. You've got good hands and a strong back—but so do half the street boys of Cape Town."

John's heart sank. "I could stow away again."

Nathaniel laughed. "Once is clever. Twice is stupid."

They sat in silence for a while. The wind came up from the sea carrying the scent of kelp and fish stew. John stared out at the vessels moored along the quay, each one a floating promise. He imagined them pushing off for unknown waters, their sails fat with the breath of destiny.

"Look," Nathaniel said after a time. "There may be a way. But you'll need to prove yourself. To Lieutenant King. To me."

"I will."

Nathaniel didn't smile. "We'll see."

That night, John walked back through the dim streets with thoughts like storm clouds. The tavern was quiet when he slipped through the side entrance. He said little to the proprietor's wife, who sat folding linens near the fire. He lay awake in the storage loft listening to the night creatures of the city—cats fighting, footsteps on cobblestone, a snore from the street below.

Back in Scotland, he believed, his mother lay dying in a cottage, waiting for a doctor's call paid for by her son. And his father—what of him? Was he drinking himself to death in some windswept alley? Did he even wonder where John had gone?

John stared into the dark. He did not cry. That part of himself had long since dried up. But he made a silent promise that night, to himself and to no one else:

He would not be left behind again. Not by death. Not by fate. If any ship left for the north coast, he would be on her. One way or another.

The *Mary* was not a ship designed to impress. She had a long, low frame, built for endurance more than elegance, and a wind-scuffed hull that looked more patched than plated. But to John Ross, who stood at the edge of the dock with Nathaniel Isaacs and squinted up at her rigging, she might as well have been a crowned frigate. This was the ship that would carry him north—toward something wilder, truer, and farther from his boyhood than even Cape Town had been. Perhaps he was about to enter the land of riches that could save his mother.

"She's old," John said of the *Mary*, trying to hide his awe.

Nathaniel smiled at him sidelong. "She's sturdy. King knows her hull like his own ribs."

"King" was Lieutenant James King, a naval man with a jaw like a winch block and a temper that flared with the same swiftness as a canvas sail catching wind. Nathaniel had introduced John to him with the barest flattery, letting the boy's lean limbs and bright eyes do most of the convincing. King had grunted, flicked a hand, and muttered something about boys being "useless until they ain't," and that was that. John was on the roster, officially as a deck runner, unofficially as the companion's shadow.

"Does he know where we're headed?" John asked, still watching the way the sails curled and flapped like breath against the sky.

"Up the Natal Coast," Nathaniel replied. "There's word of a man named Farewell—an East India merchant who vanished like smoke. And a physician too. Fynn. The last dispatch was nearly two years ago. My uncle wants to know if they're dead or just trading ivory and keeping the proceeds for themselves."

John frowned. "Sounds dangerous."

Nathaniel shrugged, but there was a light in his eye. "Which is precisely why I argued for us to go. You can't have an adventure without danger."

They boarded late in the afternoon, with gulls wailing over the harbor and stevedores shouting in a dozen tongues. The deck of the *Mary* creaked beneath John's bare feet as he followed the mate aft, eyes scanning the unfamiliar faces of the crew. Most were older, weathered men with the sea etched into their skin, but one figure stood out.

A tall African youth, no more than four or five years older than John, stood near a stack of crates, coiling rope with the ease of long practice. His build was lean but strong, his hair cropped close, and he wore a wide leather belt from which hung a sheath knife and a pouch. Around his neck, a string of polished wooden beads caught the sunlight.

"That's William," the mate said, nodding toward the youth. "Hired on as porter and interpreter. Speaks three or four tongues from up the coast, maybe more. Captain says he's worth his weight in gold when we get near Zulu lands."

John hesitated, then stepped closer. "Hello. I'm John Ross."

The young man looked up and smiled, eyes quick and friendly. "William. Just William. You new to this ship?"

John nodded. "Boarded just this morning. First time going up the Natal coast."

William gave a low whistle. "Not many want to make that journey these days. Too many stories. Too much fear."

John swallowed but said nothing.

William studied him a moment, then added, "But you look like you have reason. You travel alone?"

"Yes."

A thoughtful silence stretched between them before William nodded again. "Then we should talk more. You may need someone who knows the rivers and names and signs. Not all trouble walks with a spear."

From that moment, an understanding passed between them. Not friendship yet, but the beginning of something John could not name.

The cargo had already been mostly offloaded—textiles, coal, and gunpowder—leaving the hold echoing and dry, the way John imagined a whale's ribcage might feel from the inside. He was handed a coil of rope and told to climb the ratlines and check the mainsail rig. No instruction. No safety line. Just a bark and a stare.

John didn't blink. He leaped like a cat, his bare feet gripping the tarred ropes with practiced instinct. At the top, he turned, grinning into the wind, while the older sailors muttered something about monkeys and Highland goat-boys.

Nathaniel watched from the quarterdeck, arms crossed, and made no comment. But that night in their shared bunk, tucked just beneath the officer's cabin, he said, "You were meant for masts, John Ross. I swear it."

John stared up at the wooden slats above him. "Or perhaps I was meant for trees. Ships just got in the way."

They both chuckled.

But Nathaniel sobered after a moment. "I had a brother once," he said. "Joshua. Bit younger than you. He had red in his hair too. Bit of a temper."

"What happened?"

Nathaniel paused before answering. "Fever. Took him in under a week. Nothing we could do."

There was silence between them then—not uncomfortable, just heavy.

"I'm sorry," John said finally.

Nathaniel nodded. "I think that's part of why I wanted you aboard. You remind me a lot of him. But with more bite."

John didn't know what to say to that.

They spent the next several days helping prepare the *Mary* for departure. The harbor crew checked the lines and caulking while John learned the names of sailors and their smells—peppermint and pipe smoke, sweat and salt. One was missing half a thumb. Another had a tattoo of a kraken coiling around his neck. A third kept three gold teeth in a pouch and only wore them on Sundays.

King briefed his officers in curt tones, pointing to charts spread across a canvas roll. "There's been no word from Farewell or Fynn in a year," he said. "If they're alive, they'll be up near Port Natal, or further inland. We'll anchor when we can, trade where it's safe, and gather information. But no unnecessary risk. This is recon, not conquest."

He looked at Nathaniel and then John. "The boy keeps up, he stays. He lags, he stays behind."

John met the officer's gaze with his own. "Aye, sir. I'll keep up."

King nodded. "We'll see."

On the night before they sailed, Nathaniel took John up to the top of Signal Hill, where the stars glittered with cold brilliance and the fires and gaslights of Cape Town flickered below like embers in a hearth.

"You still want this?" Nathaniel asked.

John didn't hesitate. "I need this."

"Even if it gets dangerous?"

John looked out toward the ocean, where the black tide merged with sky and memory. "Danger's already behind me."

Nathaniel was quiet a long moment, then clapped him on the shoulder. "You're more than you seem, John Ross."

John didn't answer. He wasn't sure if he agreed yet.

The *Mary* loosed from the harbor under a wind that had teeth. Cape Town shrank behind them like a half-remembered dream, its steep hills swallowed by a veil of mist. Table Mountain loomed for a while, watching, then dissolved behind the horizon. John Ross stood at the stern rail, his fingers clenched tight around the damp wood, feeling the jolt of every swell in his knees.

There was no farewell from land. No ribboned sendoff, no waving flags. Only the squawk of gulls, the cussing of sailors, and the long groan of the brig as it shifted against the tide. But it suited John. He had no need of ceremony. His farewells had been made in the muddy back streets of Rockcliffe, in the eyes of his mother as she gave him silent permission to leave, and in the broken posture of his father after.

Now the sea. He did not yet know it was to be a hard sea.

"Wind's changing," someone called above. "Southeast squall coming!"

Lieutenant King shouted orders, and the men scrambled. John joined the rush to reef the topsail, ropes slicing through his palms as he heaved and pulled. The brig bucked and pitched like an unbroken mare. A wave slapped over the bow, sending up a surge that drenched half the crew.

John swallowed a mouthful of salt and tried not to think about throwing up.

"This isna a gentle tide," he muttered through gritted teeth.

"Don't speak ill of her," came a voice beside him—Nathaniel, bracing against the mainmast. "The *Mary's* a proud beast, and she knows when she's being mocked."

"I wasn't mocking," John said, wiping spray from his brow. "I was beggin' her mercy."

They grinned, both soaked, both shivering, but unwilling to cower. Behind them, the horizon curved like a blade, and John realized this voyage was not like stowing away on the *Annabelle*. This was no merchant's detour, no cramped escape. This was a mission into the unknown, sanctioned and paid for by men of influence, into lands that were more legend than map.

By the second day, the wind had steadied but the tension on board had not. The crew was a mix of old salts and young firebrands, and most viewed Nathaniel and John with a mix of suspicion and vague resentment. Nathaniel's position as the "companion" of the captain, especially one not drawn from naval ranks, marked him as privileged. John, as the boy who came with him, was worse—a stray.

That night, a grizzled boatswain called Big Taffy cornered John near the galley hatch.

"What're ye then?" he said. "Some fancy lad's pet? Ye bark on command or just fetch his pipe?"

John tensed. "I work my share. Same as any."

Big Taffy took a step forward. "We'll see if yer back holds when the sea throws proper. Best keep close to the rig and far from the quarterdeck, boy. Else one wave might wash ye off—"

A low voice interrupted. "If anyone's going overboard, Taffy, it'll be you."

Nathaniel didn't shout, just cleared his throat. He was standing in the shadows behind John with one hand resting calmly on the rail. But his eyes—those sharp, dark eyes—held a promise of steel.

Big Taffy spat to the side, muttered something about "land whelps," and stalked off.

John looked up. "Thanks."

"Don't thank me," Nathaniel said. "Just prove them wrong."

"I will."

Nathaniel's gaze lingered a moment. "I know."

They made anchor two weeks later in Mossel Bay, one of the last places before the coast turned rougher. Here they took on fresh water and traded for smoked fish and coarse grain. The locals spoke in Dutch-tinged Afrikaans, and John understood none of it, but watched the bartering with fascination. He had never seen black and white men trade as equals before. It unsettled him—and excited him.

From Mossel Bay they turned northeast. The coast rose and fell with jagged cliffs and hidden inlets. At night, the wind screamed through the rigging like a banshee, and John learned what it meant to fear the sea.

He also learned the quiet comfort of late-night stories.

In the cramped crew quarters, Nathaniel would sometimes speak of things John had only read in tattered volumes—temples in India, marble palaces in Persia, desert caravans in Egypt.

"My father used to say," Nathaniel murmured one night, "that the world is a puzzle box, and the only way to open it is to keep moving. Keep asking. Never settle for the lid."

John turned toward him. "Did he travel too?"

"No," Nathaniel said. "He just read. But I think I'm doing what he wished he had done."

John looked at the lantern swinging above them and casting fractured light. "Maybe I'm doin' what my da wishes he hadn't."

Nathaniel didn't speak for a long time. Then he said, "Let's make sure it matters."

By the end of the month, the *Mary* was approaching the ter- ritory of the Zulu. Rumors reached them in stops along the way—of shifting alliances, of white men who had tried to establish settlements and gone quiet. Of war camps and cattle raids. Of a land ruled not by kings, but by force.

Lieutenant King grew more terse. He came above deck only to bark orders or chart a course. He no longer spoke of Farewell or Fynn. Only "the objective." Only "the site."

John began to feel it—the press of the unknown.

He stood at the bow one night, the wind light, the water oddly calm. Stars shivered across the black surface like distant fires.

Nathaniel joined him. "Still glad you came?"

John nodded. "Aye. I just—sometimes it feels like I'm running to a place that doesn't exist."

Nathaniel leaned against the rail. "Or maybe we're running toward something waiting for us."

John turned, brow furrowed. "Ye believe that?"

"I want to."

John looked forward again. The sea didn't answer. It never did. But it listened.

CHAPTER 12

Lewis Ross had always been lean—hard-bodied from years at sea, lean-limbed from a boyhood of hunger and grit. But now, beneath the fading thatch of his hair and the pocked hollows of his cheeks, was a man disassembled. His body had been whittled by grief, sharpened by regret. The people in the village didn't even whisper about him anymore. They just turned their heads.

His days had settled into a rhythm as bitter as it was meaningless. Wake before dawn, dress slowly, feed on a crust or not at all, and drift toward the smithy just down the path from the shed where he now slept. There he moved stiffly around the forge, sweeping cinders with his one good arm and dodging the blacksmith's wary gaze. He did not complain, nor did he thank the man. He simply worked, because work was the only thing left between him and the grave.

Every evening, he walked farther than he had the day before.

It had started with a limp and a curse—his wooden leg chafing, the leather strap cruelly biting the flesh of his thigh—a kind of involuntary cilice for people of no faith. But the pain became something else in time. A punishment. A pact. A form of penance he could measure.

"Keep movin'," he muttered under his breath, sweat trickling into his eyes. "Keep movin', ye daft old fool."

By the end of the second week, he'd doubled the distance. Past the hedgerows where the cows lowed indifferently, past the crooked fence where children once jeered and threw stones. One day, he didn't hear the laughter. It took him a moment to realize the boys had stopped their taunting. They just stood there, watching him go. There was something in his eyes that chilled them.

At night, he collapsed onto the pile of straw he called a bed, his stump raw and aching. But he did not sleep easily. His dreams were full of Margaret's face, then John's. Sometimes they blurred together. Sometimes the wind sounded like their voices.

The townspeople began to take notice. He heard them whispering near the bakery: "He's walking again." And again at the well: "Did you see how he carries himself? Like a man with someplace to go."

They were right.

He did have somewhere to go, even if he didn't have an exact destination yet.

By the start of the fourth week, Lewis had begun to repair his old coat. The buttons had to be resewn. He trimmed the frayed sleeves with a knife that barely cut. He polished the brass clasp of his belt until it gleamed like a relic. He dug out his sea boots and rubbed them with pig fat to soften the leather. They still hurt, but pain was now a kind of friend.

He cut his hair with the aid of a broken mirror, the blade of a penknife trembling in his fingers. His beard he left—short and trimmed, not wild. A man didn't have to be pretty to earn his place on a ship. But he had to look the part.

It was in this condition that he went, at last, to find Captain McDugall.

Threatened docks smelled of tar, brine, and old rope. A wind rolled off the grey sea, curling under the eaves of the customs house Lewis passed the salt-weathered planks with steady steps. He kept his eyes forward, refusing to acknowledge the few who stared or nudged each other at the sight of him.

He found McDugall where he remembered—near the mooring piles, arms crossed, watching stevedores load sacks of barley into a coastal brig.

"Captain," Lewis said, his voice rough but clear.

McDugall turned, eyes narrowing at first—and then widening.

"I'll be damned," the man muttered. "Lewis Ross. I'd thought the sea had taken ye back for good."

"It nearly did." Lewis stepped forward, squared his shoulders. "But it didn't."

McDugall gave him a long look. Not cruel, not kind. Measured.

"I heard what happened. About your wife."

Lewis nodded.

"And the boy?" the captain asked.

"Gone to find somethin' I couldn't give him," Lewis replied.

McDugall grunted. "Aye. He stowed away on my ship, you know. The Annabelle."

"I know." Lewis's jaw twitched.

"You raised a clever lad. Brave, too. Earned his keep, fair and square."

Lewis didn't respond. He didn't know how. Praise for John was a blade with two edges.

"So," McDugall said slowly, "what brings ye here?"

"I want a berth."

The words landed with a silence that stretched between them.

McDugall folded his arms again. "A man with one leg and one arm walks onto my dock and says he wants a berth?"

"Aye."

"Got a crew already. Strong lads. Young."

"I won't take pay if I don't earn it."

"And what could ye do with one arm? Haul line? Climb rigging?"

"No. But I can cook. Clean. Steady a compass. Mind the helm if needed. And I've eyes that see farther than most."

McDugall raised a brow. "Ye mean to serve as cabinman?"

"I mean to prove myself. Whatever the job."

There was a pause. Then the captain's mouth twitched, almost a smile.

"Ye know," he said, "your boy said nearly the same thing. Clambered up a mast like a monkey, barefoot and wild. Nearly gave me a heart attack."

Lewis grunted.

McDugall looked him over again. This was not the broken drunk of last season, but something else now. Scarred, yes. Weathered. But anchored.

"All right," the captain said finally. "I can't promise you a voyage yet. But I've a supply run up the coast in three days. Short. You can work deck, see how you fare."

Lewis swallowed the knot in his throat. "Aye, Captain."

"Be here at dawn."

Lewis nodded and turned to leave.

"Ross," McDugall called. "You've got salt left in your bones."

Lewis gave a single nod. Then walked away.

The morning was blue with cold. Not the stinging cold of Highland winters, but the briny chill that seeps into the skin like a second tide. Lewis arrived before dawn, boots laced tight, coat buttoned high, and a wrapped parcel of bread and boiled eggs tucked under his arm. He stood at the edge of the dock, his eyes fixed on the vessel moored in shadow—the *Cormorant*, a stubby brig with tarred seams and sails still furled.

A crewman emerged from below deck, yawning.

Lewis said nothing.

Another sailor approached, chewing a hunk of cheese. He glanced at Lewis, then did a double take at the stump and peg. "You lost, old man?"

"Not lost," Lewis said calmly. "Waitin, on the captain."

McDugall arrived minutes later, his coat flaring in the wind, and gave Lewis only a nod before barking orders to the crew. "Rig the fore and haul the ballast crates! We sail with tide!"

He turned once toward Lewis and jerked his head. "You— below. Stow the rest of the dry goods in the aft galley and make sure the cook isn't still drunk."

Lewis moved. No complaints. No limp to speak of, only the thud of the wooden peg over planks. The younger men stared, but none spoke.

Down in the galley, he found a wiry cook with one lazy eye and a temper to match. The man squinted at him and said, "Don't get in my way."

"I'll clean the basin, trim the fat from that salt pork, and keep your fire lit."

The cook grunted. "Just don't burn my biscuits."

They set sail an hour later.

For the next three days, Lewis was everywhere. He polished the compass housing and secured the bunks in a gale. He caught a swinging line mid-flight with his single hand and lashed down a water barrel before it rolled clean off the stern. He managed rope knots with one arm, holding the slack in his teeth, drawing tighter loops than some of the boys twice his age.

He carried out pots of hot coffee to the crew without being asked. He hauled up a boy who slipped at the mizzen and wrapped the boy's cut hand in a clean kerchief before the boy could even start crying.

At night, while others snored in their hammocks, Lewis sat under the stars near the prow and hummed old sea songs under his breath. He didn't speak of John. But one sailor heard the name murmured once—just once—and turned away respectfully.

On the third day, they moored at a port town north of Cape Wrath to drop off grain. A longshoreman made a rude joke about "cripples in sailor's garb," and Lewis didn't even look at him—just hoisted a crate heavier than he had any business lifting and walked it calmly down the gangplank.

McDugall was watching from the quarterdeck.

That evening, after the last of the ledger was signed and the crew slouched below to rest, McDugall remained on the deck. Lewis stood nearby, wrapping a coil of rope, fingers moving slow but sure.

"Well," the captain said finally, "I'll be damned twice."

Lewis didn't turn.

"Not a complaint. Not a stumble. You even saved a boy and scrubbed the heads without being asked."

"I said I'd work," Lewis replied.

"Aye, you did. And you've earned your sea legs again. With one leg less than the rest of us." There was a pause. "I'll have a longer route next week," McDugall added, voice low. "Supply up the Skeleton Coast. Might be takin' on a few new hands. Cabin's tight, but if you want the berth—it's yours."

Lewis turned. His eyes glinted in the dimming sky. "I want it."

McDugall nodded once. "Good."

They said nothing more. But as the night came in around the *Cormorant*, and a warm breeze carried the tang of distant harbors, Lewis Ross stood at the rail and breathed deep of the air he once called home.

He stayed there long after the others had gone below, leaning on the rail with his good hand braced and the peg of his leg resting steady against the pitch-dark wood. The sea stretched ahead in sheets of silver and smoke. He thought of John—not just the boy he'd failed, but the boy he'd shaped. The boy who'd gone into the world carrying both his strength and his brokenness.

He didn't know where his son was now. Maybe never would. But somewhere in this vast, spinning world, another ship was sailing. And maybe, just maybe, a boy with too much heart and not enough years was looking up at the same stars.

Lewis touched the rim of his brow, not in salute but in remembrance. Of the wind. Of the sea. Of the man he used to be, and the one he was still becoming.

And in that quiet, salt-rinsed space between tides, Lewis Ross began to forgive himself.

CHAPTER 13

The *Mary* had been at sea nearly two weeks when the first signs of change began to creep into the men's bones. The wind, while still steady, had warmed. The tar-sealed deck, once slick with icy dew in the morning, now dried faster than the sailors could swab it. The rigging creaked louder, like joints expanding after sleep. John noticed how his shirt stuck to his back, how the salt left a fine crust on his skin, and how the stars at night burned sharper and closer than they had nearer the Cape.

John found William on the forecastle deck after dusk, seated alone with his back to the mainmast, legs drawn up beneath him. The sky overhead was brushed with faint stars, but lightning blinked in the far-off east, as if warning them of the coast they were approaching.

"You ever been this far north?" John asked, approaching with a wary step.

William nodded, slow and thoughtful. "Twice. Once with a Dutch trader. Once by foot. Long ago."

"What's it like?"

William didn't answer immediately. He pulled something from the pouch at his side—a smooth, carved token, worn by handling. He turned it in his fingers before speaking. "The land is green and quiet until it isn't. You walk a path you think is safe, then find it's already watched. The Zulu see before they're seen."

John sat down beside him, the deck still warm beneath him.

"I've heard the stories," John said. "But I don't know what's real."

"They're real," William replied. "And not all of them are just stories. Shaka's men move like smoke. They say he trains boys to run barefoot across thornbush until the blood hardens into leather. They say his warriors carry nothing but stabbing spears—no shields, no shoes, no fear."

John glanced sideways at him. "And you're not afraid?"

"I am," William said, without shame. "But fear doesn't mean I run. It means I choose carefully who I walk beside."

They sat a while longer, listening to the creak of the ship and the murmur of voices behind them. Finally, William added, "When the time comes, I'll go with you. If it's a search or a rescue, it will not be done alone."

John didn't know what to say. He simply nodded, grateful.

John had taken to sleeping on the deck when weather allowed— one eye on the sails, one ear cocked for the call of sails needing tending. It had become habit now, the rhythm of rope and canvas. Still green in his hands, but less green in his soul. Nathaniel, for his part, looked sunburned and sore but grew more certain in his bearing, less like a Londoner on adventure and more like someone who belonged.

They hadn't yet spoken much of the destination—Port Natal. It was known to some as a rumor and to others as a fool's errand. What John knew was simple—they were looking for a man who'd vanished into the wild. Two men, actually. Farewell and Fynn, names that danced on the sailors' tongues like ghost stories.

It was during one of the late suppers—little more than dry biscuit and weak broth—that the talk turned darker.

"Fynn's no doubt been eaten," grunted a heavyset man named Trigg, a seaman with hands like tree stumps and teeth missing in all the wrong places. "Mark me, lads. Zulus don't leave bones behind. Just smoke."

One of the younger men flinched. Nathaniel laughed nervously, wiping his mouth with the edge of his sleeve. "You mean the local tribes? What about them?"

Trigg raised his chin, voice lowered. "Not just tribes. *Zulus.* Shaka's men. Heard tell they don't just fight—they vanish. Smoke themselves in and out like the Devil's own ghosts. Spears curved like a hawk's beak. Shields as tall as men. And eyes—Lord above, those eyes…"

John swallowed hard. He'd heard tales back in Scotland—odd things muttered by missionaries—but they never sounded like this.

"That's nonsense," said a voice from across the barrel-table. It belonged to Adams, a lankier seaman from the East Indies. "They bleed like anyone else. Fought alongside some against the Xhosa once. They're men. Fearsome, aye—but mortal."

"Tell that to the lads who didn't come back," Trigg said.

Nathaniel leaned over to John as the others argued. "Do you believe them?"

"I don't ken what to believe," John murmured. "But I do think fear makes liars of honest men."

Still, the seed had been planted.

The days grew longer, hotter. Rations wore thin. A small leak in the hull was found and patched quickly, but not without a crew-wide inspection of every corner of the hold. Sleep came harder. One of the younger lads—Callum, barely sixteen—took ill with something feverish. The ship's medicine chest was inspected and found wanting.

Nathaniel tried to help, wetting cloth for Callum's head. "We should be better prepared," he whispered one night as they stood watch.

"We should," John agreed. "But you can't carry the world's help in a box."

The *Mary* was still sound, but the tone aboard her was shifting. Less confidence. More wary silence.

Below them, the warm seas rolled southward like molten glass.

The sun had dipped behind a copper sky when the accident occurred. It was a routine task. A sail needed reefing—wind had picked up suddenly off the starboard beam—and the topmen were called up. John went willingly. He'd taken a liking to the dizzying heights, the clarity of the air above the swaying deck. But this time, the rhythm failed. The ropes were damp with salt waster, and a careless knot had frayed.

A voice shouted below.

John looked down just in time to see the bosun, old Haines, thrown backward across the deck. A snapped rope had lashed his ankle, jerking him down. He landed hard, and the thud silenced the deck.

They got him below quickly, but his leg bent in a way it shouldn't. McDugall came to see him, face grim. No shouting, no bluster. Just a shake of the head.

"He'll be laid up," someone said. "Weeks, maybe months."

"Poor bastard," muttered another. "No ship'll take him now."

The comment reminded John of his delimbed da and how unplanned events had destroyed his life.

That night, no one spoke of reefing sails. Instead, the stories returned.

"Shaka's men'll do worse than snap a leg," said Trigg darkly. "He's got impi—warriors—trained from the time they can walk.

They don't fight for gold or kings. They fight for blood. They fight because they like to."

Nathaniel, nursing a burned hand from hauling hot tar earlier, said nothing. John watched him across the fire-barrel they'd set up near the stern for warmth. His brow was furrowed, lips tight.

Later, as they shared a small meal of salted fish, Nathaniel finally spoke. "I've heard Shaka commands more than ten thousand men. Is it true?"

"Closer to twenty, I heard in the pub," John answered. "But who's countin'? It's all guesswork once ye pass the known maps."

"But you think he's real?"

John nodded slowly. "Aye. I think there's a man behind the stories. That's the trouble, isn't it? It's easier to fight a story than a man."

Nathaniel leaned back against a coil of rope. "My brother, the one I told you about—he used to make up stories like that. Brave warriors. Jungle kings. I used to listen just to see the shape of the world he imagined."

John didn't reply for a long time. "You said he died of fever," he finally replied.

"Fever, yes" Nathaniel repeated softly. "Didn't even get a proper funeral. That's London for you. Too busy to mourn."

The wind shifted, and John pulled his blanket tighter.

"I wonder," Nathaniel said, "if this Shaka is really what they say—or just what fear needs him to be."

They watched the moon rise over the black water. The injured bosun groaned below deck. The ship creaked around them like a beast unsettled in its sleep.

And though the sea was calm, John felt the churn begin— some inner compass swaying from its fixed north.

The journey was changing. And so were they.

By the fourteenth day at sea from Cape Town, the routine aboard the *Mary* had grown brittle. What had begun with eager hands and tightened rigging now sagged under the weight of fatigue, silence and unease.

The horizon offered no promise. Only sky pressing low upon dull gray waters and the occasional jagged silhouette of coastline that flickered past and vanished.

"We shoulda seen something by now," one crewman muttered near the hold. "Too quiet. Too calm. Sea's got no right bein' this still."

The charts didn't match the coast anymore. Landmarks failed to appear where they should, and gulls flew in strange circles as if mocking the ship's course. Lieutenant King spent longer hours bent over his table, making faint notes in the margins of logbooks. He no longer offered firm predictions about when they'd reach the mythical Port Natal.

John stood with Nathaniel at the rail, watching the shoreline twist past—wild, uninhabited, and utterly alien.

"I thought we'd be among traders by now," Nathaniel said. "Or at least a settlement or two."

Adams squinted toward the land. "They say some of these coasts are empty for days. Just brush and heat and eyes watchin' from the trees."

Nathaniel lowered his voice and said to John. "Do you think the crew's right? That we're being watched?"

John didn't answer. But he remembered the way the hair on the back of his neck had risen the night before when the wind shifted and he thought he'd seen movement among the rocks. It could have been a shadow. Or it could have been a man.

That evening, one of the younger sailors, Meeks—who had been a source of comic relief since the voyage began—burst into tears during supper.

"I heard them," he whispered. "Chantin'. Out there. Voices like stone grindin'. It ain't right. We're not meant to be here."

Captain McDugall ordered silence and two hours later had Meeks placed on deck patrol. But no one laughed.

The ship grew quieter, the usual banter halted. The men began carrying knives tucked in their boots. They whispered about a tribe called the Qwabe, rumored to have traded lives for steel along this coast. Others argued they'd already passed into Zulu territory, and that Shaka's warriors might be waiting at Port Natal—if not sooner.

Nathaniel tried to distract himself with reading, but the salt air had bloated the pages of his journal. He stared at his ink-smudged reflections and finally tossed the journal aside.

"I'm not afraid of stories," he said to John one morning.

"No?" John answered, lashing a coil of rope to the side rail. "Maybe you should be. Some stories are maps. They tell ye where not to go."

That night, the storm began—not the ship-breaking kind, but a long, slow battering from the southeast, full of sand and wet heat. The sails had to be trimmed constantly, the watch rotated faster. Tempers rose. Salt got into every joint. The deck creaked as though the ship herself disapproved of the voyage.

Still no sign of Port Natal.

Just jungle hills rising in the distance and the ever-deepening weight of the journey.

They were somewhere now that the maps had stopped describing. A land charted only in warning and tale.

The storm passed in its own good time—three days of soaked canvas and red eyes—but it left the *Mary* in calmer seas and closer to shore. By the morning of the fourth day, a pale band of beach stretched northward like a beckoning road, and hills rolled inland under mist like the backs of sleeping beasts.

The captain let the men breathe. Cook fires were lit early. Even the rats grew bold enough to show their snouts again. But the relief didn't last long.

A man named Crawley—a wiry, sea-bitten old mariner with cheeks like bark—told a story as they ate salted fish that night. The story gripped the deck like wind in the sails.

"Saw 'em once, ten years past. Zulu raiders. They don't wear armor. Don't need it. Just spears, shields, and silence. And they run. Run like lions do—quiet, fast, then all at once."

"Met 'em where?" someone asked.

"Drakensberg side. I was with a Dutch trader then, name of Pieter. Fool went inland with beads and a musket. We never found his bones. Only his boots."

A younger crewman laughed, but it died in his throat when Crawley leaned in. "You think Shaka's just a chief? He's not. He's a ghost walking. They say he dreams war and his dreams come true. He eats other kings for breakfast."

John listened without comment, pretending not to care—but later, in the dark, he asked Nathaniel, "Do you believe any o' that?"

Nathaniel stared at the stars, the clearest they'd been in weeks. "Some of it. Not the ghost part. But Shaka… I've read his name in reports. He's not fiction."

"What if we meet 'em?"

"Then we better know why we came."

John didn't reply, because he didn't know—not fully. At first it had been about running. Then about money. Then about not going home. Now it was something else. He didn't know what.

Two days later, sails were spotted on the southern horizon. The *Mary's* lookout raised the alarm, and Lieutenant King was summoned. But the sails never approached. They vanished as quickly as they came, and no one could tell if they were Dutch, English—or something else.

Nathaniel grew more anxious with each mile.

"They should've sent word by now. Farewell's camp was supposed to have posted letters every quarter. There's been nothing. My uncle said eighteen months since a word was heard."

"They could be fine," John offered. "Out huntin'. Or buildin'."

"Or just gone," Nathaniel said. "Like the ones Crawley talked about."

That night, Nathaniel tried to write another letter home but tore the paper in frustration.

Meanwhile, another story made the rounds below deck. This one from a stowaway-turned-sailor who claimed to have seen a Zulu trial of fire—young warriors forced to run through thorn beds and ash until only one emerged. That one, the story went, would be sent to kill his own brother as a test of loyalty.

"Is it true?" John whispered.

"Even if it's not," Nathaniel answered, "someone believes it. That's enough."

By the time the wind turned west again, Port Natal still hadn't appeared, and food was growing sparse. Insects regularly launched raiding parties against the crew. The coastal air was humid, sickly. Men began coughing, especially the older ones. It seemed the land wanted nothing from them—no trade, no talk, no treaty.

Only silence.

On the seventh night after the storm, the *Mary* dropped anchor near a sandbar for the first time since leaving Algoa Bay. It was a test run, a planned rest before they sailed into the inlet they hoped was Port Natal.

But the next morning, something went wrong.

John awoke to shouting, men running, sails flapping loose. A crewman had spotted a shifting shoal, too close. McDugall gave sharp orders, and the rudder cracked under strain. The ship lurched—once, twice—and then held.

They hadn't wrecked. Not yet. But the *Mary* groaned in protest and listed hard to starboard.

That's when John saw it—not a wave, not a rock—but smoke. A thin trail curling from inland trees.

"Do you see it?" he asked.

Nathaniel followed his gaze. "Yes."

"Think it's them?"

Nathaniel didn't answer. Not yet.

They would anchor there another day. By the next morning, the tide would answer that question for them.

CHAPTER 14

They let Lewis off the *Annabelle* for a single day before final provisioning. Captain McDugall said it was standard. "Settle your affairs. Be back on deck by dawn or she sails without you."

The air ashore felt different. As if the sea had marked him.

Lewis Ross walked with a slower tread than he had just a week before. He moved with the balance of a man who'd relearned the ship's rhythm and had now found the land unsteady. His clothes were the same—patched jacket, fraying collar—but he wore them in a different manner. Shoulders straighter. Chin less tethered to the dirt.

The dockhands didn't greet him by name, but they no longer stared like they used to.

He passed the blacksmith's lane just as Muir stepped out, arms black with soot. The man paused, hammer still in hand, and gave a gruff nod.

"You're shipping out, then?" he asked.

Lewis nodded. "Tomorrow."

Muir wiped his forehead with a sleeve. "To find the boy?"

"To find something," Lewis said. "And maybe him, if I can."

Muir didn't argue with the odds. Didn't say what the village priest had said the week prior—that Africa was a death sentence for old men with sins to outrun. Instead, he stepped back and opened the forge door.

"Come," he said. "You'll need something sturdier than what's on your feet."

An hour later, Lewis left with a pair of hobnailed boots, slightly too big but near-new, and a small pouch of iron nails "just in case." He offered to pay, but Muir waved it off.

"Use the coin to stay alive down there," the smith muttered. "I hear it gets hot enough to melt sense right out of your skull."

Lewis turned at the lane's end and raised a hand in thanks. It wasn't quite a farewell. Just something close.

The wind along the bluff was sharp, the kind that bit your face and chapped your lips no matter how tight you wrapped your collar. Lewis stood just off the path, where the thistles grew high and ragged, looking up at the old Ross cottage.

He hadn't been back since the landlord had thrown him out.

The thatched roof sagged now in places, and a fresh shutter had been nailed across one of the windows. The owner had seen fit to erase what was left of his past.

He stood there a long time, cap in hand, watching the smoke curl from a distant chimney. Not *his*. Not anymore.

It had been Margaret's dying place. And John's childhood.

And his own ruin.

He didn't try to go closer. Just stared until his eyes stung— not from wind, not just from grief, but from the awful weight of knowing that nothing in that house, or in the world, still belonged to him.

He turned to go, his boots crunching frostbitten leaves. That's when Doctor Cargill stepped from the bend in the path, wrapped in a dark coat, carrying a letter and a walking stick.

"I was hoping I'd find you here," the doctor said quietly.

Lewis tipped his head, but didn't speak.

Cargill held out the envelope. "No word of your boy, but I thought you might want this. It's the last letter Margaret ever wrote. She gave it to my daughter when she was too weak to hold a pen."

Lewis took it slowly, staring at the creases in the paper. He didn't open it.

"She wrote it for you," Cargill said. "Before she knew if you'd ever come back."

Lewis nodded sadly. "Thank you."

They stood in silence, two men with nothing more to offer each other. Then Lewis asked, "Do you think he's alive? John, I mean."

Cargill looked out toward the grey sea without answering. Finally, he said, "I think sons carry more of us than we deserve. And if he is alive, he's likely out there looking for what you never gave him."

Lewis looked down at the letter again. "Then I'll find him before the weight turns him bitter."

He tucked the envelope into his coat and walked away, not once turning back to look at the cottage.

The wind came hard off the Firth that morning, flattening the waves into slate ridges and throwing the gulls into looping cries. Lewis stood on the deck of the *Annabelle* just before dawn, his boots braced against the roll and his hands closed around the rail.

They were preparing to cast off. The sails hung ready, furled like clenched fists above them. The crew moved with quickened purpose, calling out in low Scots and short curses. A final barrel was rolled aboard. The anchor creaked upward.

Captain McDugall moved like a man who had done this a thousand times. "Stand ready for wind!" he barked. "She'll pull left as we clear the harbor mouth."

Lewis didn't speak. He felt the thrum of it all through his soles—the swell of the water under hull, the shuddering release as the *Annabelle* slid free of land. No one watched from the quay. No one waved. That suited him fine.

The sails cracked once, then spread open like wings. The ship tilted into her first true tack, and Lewis saw the coastline fall away— the low hills, the chimney smoke, the path that led to the bluff. It all shrank behind them like something imagined.

He didn't look back a second time.

The first week aboard was hard. His hands, soft from too many empty days, blistered and split open on the lines. The salt burned the raw spots until they crusted, then peeled again. His back protested the weight of the barrels he helped lash down. The motion of the ship at night made sleep a strange and fragile thing.

But he worked.

McDugall noticed. He said nothing, but nodded once when Lewis climbed the rigging without flinching on the fourth morning. The other men—most of them younger—grumbled at first, then accepted him. You didn't argue with a man who kept pace, and Lewis did.

He spoke little. But he listened.

He learned the shape of the *Annabelle's* moods—the creak she made when tacking hard into a north wind, the way her hull whispered when night fogs set in, the gull-patterns that told when fish ran close beneath. These small things mattered. They made the sea feel less like exile and more like ritual.

It helped that the weather held.

They sailed south past Biscay with only a brief squall. No one was washed over. No sails split. McDugall said it was the cleanest passage he'd had in months.

But Lewis knew that even calm seas couldn't quiet a storm already inside you. He kept the letter folded in his jacket. At night, when the men slept in swinging hammocks and the lantern above creaked with the ship's sway, he'd reach for it. But he never opened it. Just pressed it between his palms like a prayer not yet said.

One evening, while coiling rope on the quarterdeck, a deckhand named Sheamus sidled up beside him. He was only a few years older than John, with a broken tooth and a voice like gravel soaked in rum.

"She said anything to you, your Margaret?"

Lewis looked over slowly.

"The letter," Sheamus added, jerking his chin. "I seen you holding it sometimes."

Lewis was quiet a long while before saying, "Not yet."

Sheamus nodded like he understood. "Sometimes they don't come through till you're ready."

They didn't speak again that night.

The sun was a white disc in a blank sky when the first fin sliced the surface.

Lewis had been watching the water as he often did in the afternoons, coiling rope or rinsing salt from his sleeves. The others laughed and played dice in the shade of the aft sail, but Lewis stood alone at the rail. That was when he saw it—just a shimmer, a glint of motion, then the unmistakable curve of a dorsal fin cutting like a blade through the calm.

Another. Then two more.

Sharks.

The deck tilted slightly, but Lewis's knees locked as if the ship had lurched. His breath vanished. He gripped the rail with both hands and leaned forward, peering into the blue churn. The creatures circled lazily below, not hunting—just present. As if waiting.

He couldn't move. The fear was instant, as if it had never left him. The memory of that reef in his youth, the blood in the water, the stories told on storm-nights about bones picked clean in seconds—it all rose in him like bile. His lungs burned. The rails seemed thinner. The deck less sure.

He didn't realize he'd staggered until a rope-end caught his boot.

"You all right there, Ross?" Sheamus called from the shade.

Lewis nodded too quickly. "Just the heat."

But it wasn't the heat. It was the things in the water. The things in his mind.

He turned from the rail, sat on a barrel, and pressed his hands to his knees until they stopped shaking. He muttered a prayer—not to be spared, but to be calmed. The difference mattered.

The storm came three days later. It didn't roar in with trumpets or lightning—it crept. The clouds gathered low and slow like a tide of ash, blotting the sun by mid-morning. The air changed first—thick, metallic, almost still. Birds vanished. The sea flattened, eerie and glass-dark.

"Something's wrong with the wind," McDugall said at noon, staring at the sky.

By late afternoon, the color had gone out of everything. The horizon looked bruised. Men spoke in whispers now, the way they might near a deathbed.

Then came the first squall.

A shudder ran through the mast as rain lashed the deck in slanting sheets. The sails were reefed in haste, the boom tied down. The *Annabelle* groaned, resisting.

And then the sea rose.

It rose not in waves but in walls, green and black and shifting. Thunder cracked behind it like a bone breaking. The wind shrieked so high it stopped sounding like wind and became something else— like screaming.

Lewis tied himself to the railing with a length of tarred rope, working by instinct. Beside him, Sheamus shouted something, but the words tore away into the gale. They were blind in spray. Men vanished and reappeared in the bursts of white-capped fury, the deck a chaos of motion and sound.

Night fell with no dusk between. The storm had swallowed the sun. Only flashes of lightning gave shape to the world—jagged glimpses of a sea gone mad, of canvas torn like paper, of faces locked in terror.

Lewis moved with the ship. He didn't think. He climbed, braced, hauled rope, screamed warning. He bled from his hand and didn't notice. The storm had become everything.

And then, without warning, the wind broke.

A hole opened in the sky.

The rain softened.

The men paused, panting, soaking wet. Above them, a sliver of stars emerged, faint and trembling. The *Annabelle* rocked gently on the spent breath of the sea.

"It's over," someone called.

Lewis turned, hard to his brow, searching for McDugall. He never saw the line.

A coil of rigging, loosened in the fury, whipped free and caught his shoulder. He twisted, stumbled—and was gone over the side.

The ocean hit him like stone. Then silence. A bone-deep silence that cracked his ribs and filled his ears with pressure and cold. He tumbled, spinning end over end, blind in the dark rush of sea. The world was gone—ship, sky, direction. Only the crush of water and the deafening absence of breath.

He broke the surface with a desperate gasp, flailing his one arm instinctively. Salt stung his mouth. He coughed, choked, fought for air. The *Annabelle* loomed nearby, massive and moving, blurred through spray and foam.

"Man overboard!" someone was yelling. "Ross is over!"

A rope flew past his head, but he didn't reach for it. Not yet. Because something else moved beneath him. The water, warm now from adrenaline and fear, was no longer empty.

He felt it before he saw it.

That shift. That displacement of water below, the subtle heave that had nothing to do with waves.

His breath caught mid-chest. His legs stopped kicking.

Then—there.

A fin.

It surfaced twenty yards to his left. Sleek, black, effortless. A second one followed, and a third. Slow arcs around him, slipping just below the waterline like knives through silk.

His limbs froze.

His throat sealed shut.

The old fear returned again—not as a thought, but as a seizure of the soul.

One shark passed so close beneath him that the ridge of its back kissed the sole of his boot. The water around it dimpled in its wake.

He screamed—but the sound came out small and strangled.

The *Annabelle* swayed in and out of focus, ropes trailing. McDugall's voice echoed from above, muffled by the distance between life and death. "Grab the line, Ross! Grab it, now!"

He tried.

His one arm moved like lead.

Another fin surfaced. This one was larger. It turned in a lazy circle, and for a moment, Lewis could see its eye. Not wild. Not angry. Just calm, unblinking, eternal.

Predatory.

The water pulsed. Then stilled. They were circling him now.

He turned in place, spinning slowly, trying to see them all. Impossible. They moved like spirits, visible only when they chose to be seen. He kicked once with his peg, then stopped. He remembered that splashing drew them closer.

His breath came ragged. The water pressed in around him, thick and endless. His arm began to shake.

"I don't want to die like this," he said aloud, though the words vanished into the sea.

Then the nearest one turned. It moved with sudden precision, sleek tail cutting hard left. A ripple. A surge forward.

It was coming.

Lewis braced for the pain, for the feel of teeth. Time slowed to a crawl. Every nerve in his body lit up.

But the shark passed inches beneath him and vanished.

Lewis didn't breathe. He didn't blink.

And then something touched his boot.

It was the tail of the smaller shark—just a brush—but it sent panic crashing through him like lightning. His good leg kicked. His body flailed.

A mistake. They turned toward him again.

He screamed once more. This time, the sound tore from his throat, raw and high and human. A man unmade. A soul unraveling.

He looked upward—toward the faint shape of the *Annabelle*, toward the sky, toward whatever power ruled the water and the wind.

"God—please," he choked.

A fin broke the surface ten feet away.

He was going to die. Here. Like this.

Then—

A rope.

It struck his shoulder. Heavy. Soaked.

A second later: "Lewis! Grab it! Now!"

He turned—blind with salt and terror—and lunged.

His fingers missed.

The rope slapped the water again, curling.

The fin came closer.

He screamed. Swung his arm wildly. Caught the rope.

He gripped with everything he had. His hand burned.

"Pull him! Pull!"

The rope went taut, his body dragged sideways, then upward. His peg kicked off one of the sharks. He felt the tail brush his shin.

He rose.

The hull scraped his back. A hand reached down—Sheamus, eyes wide with panic—and grabbed his collar. Another hand. King's voice barking.

They hauled him over the rail in one brutal jerk.

He collapsed onto the deck, coughing, retching seawater, his whole body convulsing. He could still feel them below—still see that eye.

Silence fell. Only the creak of the rigging and the soft hush of wind remained.

The storm was gone. The sea had calmed. But Lewis Ross was shaking with something deeper than cold.

The captain crouched beside him. "You all right, Ross?"

Lewis couldn't speak.

Not for a long time.

That night, after dry clothes and silence and the warmth of a small blanket below deck, Lewis sat in the corner of the crew quarters. No one joked. No one mocked. Even Sheamus looked at him like a man come back from death.

Lewis reached into his coat and pulled out Margaret's letter. He unfolded it with care, then read every word. And when he finished, he looked up at the single round porthole and saw the stars again.

"I should've died," he whispered.

But he hadn't.

Something had watched. Something had spared him. And in that truth—awful, humbling, holy—Lewis felt no fear.

Only the quiet, ringing promise of what still waited ahead.

CHAPTER 15

The morning after the grounding of the *Mary* came heavy and wet, the sun rose slowly behind gauze-thick cloud. Mist clung to the sea like sweat, and the shallows around the brig steamed as if the ocean had been wounded and was still trying to breathe.

John Ross stood amidships, his hand gripping the damp rail. The deck tilted underfoot—not violently, but wrong, like a hip out of its socket. Around him, the men moved with a kind of brittle efficiency—quiet voices, open eyes, boots thudding on soaked timber. It had been a bad night.

From shore, the jungle watched them.

To the untrained eye, the ship looked intact—leaning but proud. But as the tide drew away and the first rays of sun slipped over the trees, the truth revealed itself like rot beneath bark.

"Rudder's cracked clear through," Lang the carpenter muttered, wading in water up to his thighs. "Port strake's twisted out. We're buckled at the keel."

Lieutenant King stood on the quarterdeck with arms folded, jaw set like iron. "She'll float," he said.

"Aye," Lang replied, squinting up. "So does driftwood."

There was a silence then. The kind that made a crew go still.

"What about repair?" someone asked.

Lang shook his head. "We'd need a full drydock, a new rib frame, fresh tar, pitch rope, a month at least, and a miracle."

John didn't speak. He was watching the shoreline again, still spooked by the smoke seen the previous evening.

By midmorning, they were offloading the essentials—barrels, crates, sailcloth, salted meat and tools.

Among the crew, William moved easily between tasks, lifting and sorting with a quiet efficiency that drew no complaints. He spoke little, but when he did, it was in low, measured tones—in Zulu to one man, in passable Dutch to another. John watched him direct two of the younger hands toward a stack of soaked crates, his gestures precise and patient. It struck John that the man seemed to carry his knowledge like a compass—never pointing at himself, but always guiding others.

They hadn't spoken much since boarding, but William had nodded to him that morning and offered a half smile. Now, as they worked the surf line, he paused near John.

"Sea gives, sea takes," William murmured, glancing at the wreckage washing ashore.

John looked up, uncertain whether to reply.

William continued, "But this land... it listens. You just need to know what to say."

Then he moved off again, leaving John with the distinct impression that he wasn't just talking about the sea or the land—but about the journey ahead.

The beach was narrow, sloping up toward dry land shaded by tall knobthorn trees. Mosquitos already whined at their ears. William slapped at his neck and muttered something under his breath in a language John didn't recognize. He'd taken to carrying one of the smaller crates single-handedly, navigating the slippery sand with quiet efficiency. Though he rarely spoke unless addressed, John had noticed how the other porters deferred to him, as if he already knew more of the land than any map could teach.

The surgeon's face went pale when he opened the medicine chest—seawater everywhere, bottles smashed or soaked through.

"Gone," he whispered. "The quinine's dust. The laudanum's spoiled. We've got little more than bandages and spirit vinegar."

King didn't curse. He just nodded once and said, "Set up shade on the high ground. We'll need shelter before the rains."

That was when John saw it again. A thin pillar of smoke, faint, curling above the trees inland—not far. It was not the angry black of firewood or battle. It was clean and white, steady. Intentional.

Nathaniel appeared beside him. "Still burning," he murmured. "I saw it last evening too."

John nodded. "Too far for us. Too close to ignore."

King followed their gaze. "That direction," he said quietly. "That's where Farewell and Dr. Fynn were meant to be operating."

Nathaniel turned to face him. "You think it's them?"

The captain didn't answer. Instead, he called for four men—Lang, Sheamus, a wiry Dutchman named Liam, and John. Nathaniel volunteered before King could object.

"You know the terrain?" the captain asked him.

"No," Nathaniel said. "But I know what to look for."

King nodded once. "Take arms. Minimal packs. Be back by nightfall or send smoke of your own. If it's Farewell, we'll need his help. If it's not…"

He let the words hang.

They set out through the undergrowth by late morning. Heat pressed in like wool soaked in soup. Vines tugged at their boots. The buzz of unseen insects swelled and broke like surf.

They found an animal track, old and sunken, and followed it inland. The smoke thinned, barely visible now behind a stand of trees. But the sense of being observed never left them.

Birds went quiet. A bushbaby shrieked once, then fell silent.

Nathaniel crouched near a print in the mud—hooved, wide, but blurred by rain. "Cattle," he said. "Zebu or Nguni, likely herded."

John knelt beside him. "Zulu?"

Nathaniel stood. "Could be. Could be others. But someone lives here. Someone who moves with intention."

Sheamus said, "I don't like walking into smoke we didn't light."

Lang raised a hand. "Quiet. Hear that?"

No one did. And that was the problem.

They pushed deeper into the lowland thicket, the heat now rising like a tide off the black earth. Mosquitos clouded the air, and once, Liam smacked his neck and muttered something in Dutch that sounded like a curse. The light changed with every step—green-gold shafts through thorn and palm, shadows draped across strange roots.

John's shirt clung to his spine. His eyes burned from sweat.

Then, the scent changed. Not woodsmoke. Something sharper. Acrid, mineral—bone ash or charred hide.

Lang signaled for a halt.

They came upon the first circle just past a ridge of termite mounds. It was no firepit. Charcoal blackened the soil in a perfect ring nearly ten feet across. At its center, the earth was scorched white. Around the edges, someone—many someones—had driven short wooden poles upright, each wrapped with a twist of braided grass. Chicken feathers clung to a few. There was a line of small stones running inward in a spiral. No footprints nearby.

"What the devil is this?" Sheamus whispered.

Nathaniel crouched, studying it. "Ritual," he said. "I've read of Zulu purification ceremonies. Sometimes they burn ground to cleanse it. This spiral here—it's not random. Might be part of a spiritual boundary. Or a warning."

Liam took a step back.

John stared at the circle. "Why here?"

"Could be sacred ground," Nathaniel replied. "Or a marker to keep others out. Or in."

Lang knelt and picked up one of the stones. It was smoothed river-rock, but the side facing down had a streak of dried ochre—painted intentionally.

"This isn't a cooking fire," he muttered.

"No," Nathaniel said. "This is a message."

They moved on.

Another hundred yards inland, they found what remained of the encampment.

Canvas torn loose, stakes collapsed, a single cracked crate with shattered glass jars inside—empty medicine vials. A journal, pages water-stained and gnawed by insects. But no bodies. No blood. Signs of life, though, that had once been there—two hammocks strung haphazardly between trees, footprints trailing in several directions, and the unmistakable smell of old gunpowder.

"Farewell and Fynn," Nathaniel said. "This had to be their station."

John picked up the journal and turned the pages carefully. On one, scrawled in ink now gone faint, he could make out a partial line: *"...negotiations strained... interpreter refused..."*

Another: *"...Zulu emissaries arrived unarmed..."*

John looked up sharply. Nathaniel met his gaze.

"They made contact," John said.

"Looks like it," Nathaniel whispered. "But something went wrong."

Liam whistled.

They turned. Liam was pointing toward the edge of the clearing.

There, at the forest's edge, sat a small cookfire—cold now, but surrounded by blankets folded with care. Two carved wooden bowls, untouched. A walking stick carved with a Zulu spiral.

Then the bushes moved, and out came two men—dark-skinned, barefoot, shaking. One collapsed immediately. The other stood for a moment, staring with hollow eyes. His clothes were tattered, his face smeared with dried mud and blood.

He spoke first in isiZulu. Then again, faltering, in Englis. "They took them. The king's men. They say he wanted words."

Nathaniel stepped forward gently. "Farewell? Dr. Fynn? They're alive?"

The man nodded slowly. "Taken," he said again. "To the man with eyes like fire. You must not follow."

The other porter moaned in the dirt, clutching his belly. Fever, possibly worse.

Sheamus turned to Lang. "What now?"

Lang looked at the jungle, then back at the men.

"We carry them back," he said. "Then tell Lieutenant King what we found. And pray to God we're not next."

John glanced at the journal again.

"...they say he wants words..."

But words, John thought, weren't always what a king demanded.

CHAPTER 16

The dying porter moaned again. He lay on a makeshift cot of sailcloth stretched between two branches, his skin slick with sweat, lips cracked from thirst.

A few yards off, William helped rig a sunshade using spare canvas and driftwood poles, working without being asked. He kept glancing toward the injured men with a pinched expression—worried but quiet about it. Since landing, he'd moved like someone used to improvising, calm even amid the confusion. John noted it, filed it away. William wasn't loud, but he was present—and that counted for something.

The other porter, older and more lucid, sat cross-legged near the fire, his eyes hollow but alert. John crouched beside him, holding a battered canteen. The porter took it with trembling fingers and drank slowly, watching the boy over the rim.

Nathaniel knelt across from them, notebook in hand. He wanted to document everything the porter said. The older man spoke in slow, clipped English.

"We were left. After they were taken."

"Taken by whom?" Nathaniel asked.

"Warriors. From the mountains. Not many first time. Just seven. No spears drawn." He closed his eyes a moment, steadying himself. "Doctor try to speak. Offer salt. Pipes. But leader say nothing. Just point east. Say the king wants words. No choice."

"Was there violence?"

The porter shook his head. "Not then. But after, others come. Not to talk."

John's gut tightened.

Nathaniel nodded. "A second group?"

"They take what is left. Smash pots. Burn crates. Make fire circles." He hesitated. "We think... warning us."

The other porter groaned louder now. His body began to seize, and John jumped back. Nathaniel dropped the notebook and called for Sheamus. Minutes later, the man was dead.

Nathaniel stood silently as Sheamus and two sailors carried the body away. John looked over to see Liam, the Dutchman, staring out toward the jungle.

Lieutenant King, standing just inside the ring of firelight, finally spoke. "These natives took them to meet a king," he said slowly, "but what sort of king sends fire and ash to parley?"

No one answered.

King stepped closer, adjusting his coat, sea salt crusted across the collar. "Do you know what we're looking at here?" he said. "Shaka is no backcountry warlord. This Zulu monarch—he's something else entirely. I heard about him from a Dutch trader at Simon's Town. Regiments, discipline, ranks like Napoleon. Some say he's got maybe twenty thousand spears under his command."

John frowned. "That many?"

"Or more," King said. "And if he's dragging British traders into the bush to 'speak,' what do you suppose he'll do when more settlers arrive? Mark my words—this won't stay local. If London catches wind of this, they'll have no choice but to act."

"Send troops?" Nathaniel asked.

"I'd wager they're already considering it," King replied. "You don't let savages raise a kingdom while you're still building outposts."

Liam turned at that. "You'll stir panic with such talk."

"I'm not here to soothe nerves," King snapped. "I'm here because the Crown pays me to assess risk. And right now, the risk is staring us in the face."

No one argued further.

The porter by the fire closed his eyes and said softly, "The king will not forget who steps on his soil."

Silence wrapped the camp. Even the insects seemed to hush.

Nathaniel looked over at John, then at the flickering jungle. He had the sense that they were no longer merely guests here. They were being watched. Judged.

And somewhere beyond the veil of green, a man with fire in his eyes waited.

The first man to fall was Morris, a thick-shouldered Welshman who had served as sailmaster aboard the *Mary*. By the end of the second day after the porters returned, he was raving with fever.

"Sheamus says he's taken something foul through the water," Nathaniel muttered, helping John rig a sheet between two crates to shade the sick.

"Didn't we boil it?"

"We tried. Not enough wood for long enough, maybe. Or maybe it's from the meat we pulled off the wreck. Too long in the sun."

Morris moaned and turned over, clawing at his chest. Blisters were forming under his arms.

By nightfall, two more were down—a pale apprentice named Hall and one of the rigging hands who'd taken a scratch from coral.

The ship's surgeon, Mr. Albright, knelt beside them with trembling hands. His field kit had been soaked and ruined days ago. The vials of quinine were spoiled, the surgical tools rusted. His opium tincture had been poured into the sand, mistaken for rotgut.

"I can give them willow bark tea," he said to the captain in frustration, "and prayers."

"That'll have to do," King replied.

They moved the sick to the far end of the camp, uphill, near a stand of marula trees. Smoke from the cooking fire still reached them, but the breeze turned midday and began carrying a stench of bile back down to the others.

John helped where he could—carrying wood, boiling cloths, listening to Albright's terse instructions. But the helplessness, the *wait*, wore heavier than any chore.

By the third day, Hall had died. The crew's mood shifted with his last breath. A subtle hardening. Liam stopped joking. Nathaniel no longer kept notes.

Some of the men whispered about leaving the camp and heading west toward known settlements—or at least inland water. "Better to walk than rot," someone muttered when they thought John couldn't hear.

Liam, when asked, only scowled. "You want to die faster, go ahead. The coast at least gives you fish and firewood."

But the fish weren't biting. Nets hung empty. Crabs were scarce. The salted pork was nearly gone, and what hardtack remained was crawling with weevils.

A party was sent up the hill with muskets and blades. They returned three hours later with two scrub hares, a stringy bush pigeon, and wild guavas the size of thumbs.

"It'll feed six," one of them muttered.

Nathaniel tried to forage for medicinal roots, but his knowledge was limited. He boiled leaves that smelled promising. Albright sniffed and tossed them aside. "Would do more good as mulch."

One morning, as the sun punched low over the sea, John walked the beach alone. His stomach twisted with hunger. His hands shook not from exertion but from wear.

He stopped by the tide line and looked at the sea. Waves rolled soft and steady. The sky above was blistering blue. It should have been beautiful. Instead, it felt like the edge of a grave.

Behind him, a man vomited. Another cried out for his mother.

And still, no sign of Farewell. No word from Fynn. No path forward but guesswork and grit.

John stood alone for a long time. And then turned back toward camp, jaw clenched, boots sinking into the soft sand with every step.

By the sixth night, no one slept easy. Even the wind had turned strange. It moaned low through the branches in pulses, like breath. A fog had drifted in from the east, clinging to the trees at dawn and not lifting until midday. The beachflies multiplied. And somewhere just beyond the ridge, they began to hear it—

Drumming.

Faint. Measured. A low, rhythmic thudding that seemed to rise from the belly of the earth and echo across the canopy.

At first, it came only at dusk. Then it returned at noon. Then midnight.

Sheamus blamed the heat. Albright said dehydration could cause auditory hallucinations.

But John had sharp ears, and he wasn't the only one. "It's no echo," he whispered to Nathaniel one morning, "and not a bird, either."

They were up early, helping Liam sort through salvage under a tarp stretched between two branches. Nathaniel nodded grimly.

"I heard it last night too. It stopped just before the tide turned."

That day, Lieutenant King gave orders for another search party—this one larger, better armed, and instructed to follow the smoke trails inland and loop toward where the porters said Farewell's last camp had been.

Lieutenant King led them, with Nathaniel among the volunteers. John asked to go, but King refused.

"You're thirteen and half-starved," the captain said bluntly. "And I need you here to help Liam manage the stores."

"But I know the jungle better than most—"

"You know fog and roots. Not what lies beyond. You'll get your turn soon enough."

John bit his tongue. He didn't say what he was thinking—that he felt useless here, that the air pressed too tight against his ribs, that he needed to *move*, to *do*, or he'd rot like the sick.

The party left by noon, eight men armed with muskets, machetes and knives, along with two porters to follow the trail. They moved inland in silence, swallowed by green.

Back at camp, the hours dragged on.

Liam spent the afternoon fashioning a fish trap out of mangled rigging. Sheamus tried boiling palm hearts, but they turned bitter. John climbed a tree and saw nothing but haze in every direction.

But at dusk, just as the sky went molten and the surf turned black, he spotted it. A flicker of white deep in the tree line.

It vanished quickly, but it wasn't a trick of the eye. It was too solid, too upright.

Not animal. Not mist.

A figure. Watching.

John slid down the tree and ran for camp, breath ragged.

By the time he reached Liam, the man was stoking coals. "Easy, lad, what's in you?"

"Someone's out there," John gasped. "Watching us. I swear it."

Liam didn't laugh. He set down the stick and rose, brushing his hands on his coat.

"Then we keep the fires high tonight," he said. "And double the watches."

"But—what if they're Zulus?"

Liam looked toward the darkened trees, then back at John.

"Then we pray they're only watching. And not counting."

CHAPTER 17

The *Annabelle* rounded the curve of Robben Island at dawn, the sea bronzed by the rising sun. Lewis Ross stood near the bow, hands gripping the worn rail, eyes fixed on the mountainous landmass ahead. Table Mountain loomed in the distance—its flat summit cast in shadow as though it wore a crown of ash. Cape Town stirred beneath it, quiet at first, then slowly gaining activity. Sail-rigged vessels rocked in the harbor, flags unfurled, cargo hoisted by men with skin of many shades.

It was not the first time Lewis had laid eyes on the Cape. Years ago, during his merchant days, he'd passed through this port—but it had meant little to him then. Now, every building, every flagpole and figure on the quay shimmered with the possibility of news. News of his boy.

Captain McDugall, heavyset and sunburned, stepped up beside him. "Don't expect much grace from the customs lot. But I've a friend at the dockmaster's office. He might smooth things."

Lewis gave a distracted nod. He barely heard the man. In his pocket, folded into a square no larger than his palm, was the letter Margaret had written to him on her deathbed. It crinkled when he moved, a paper heart beating next to his own. That letter, and the long months at sea, had taught him more about time than he'd learned in fifty years. Time could collapse, stretch, vanish—and return like a ghost.

When the ship docked, the smells of salt, tar and spice assaulted his nose. Rows of ox-drawn wagons lined the harbor road. Slaves and freedmen carried barrels and crates while colonial officials in sun-bleached uniforms barked orders. Traders wore linen or tattered wool, and the air hung heavy with language—Arabic, Portuguese, Dutch. Cape Town was a city built on layers, and Lewis felt like a ghost moving through its edge.

He walked away from the ship without a word, knapsack slung over one shoulder, boots stirring dust from cobblestones. He avoided the polished colonial storefronts and instead followed the harbor road to a rougher quarter of town where sailors brawled outside rum-stained doorways and dogs nosed through scraps in the street.

He stopped outside a crooked-shingled building. The faded sign read *The Fisher's Mug*. This is the kind of place where a boy with no money might find work—and trouble—especially a boy with work experience in such a place. He stepped inside.

The interior was dim, thick with the smell of pipe smoke and yeast. A woman stood behind the counter, her graying hair coiled under a kerchief. She eyed him warily.

"Help you, sir?" she asked.

Lewis removed his cap. "I'm looking for someone. A boy. Red-haired, about thirteen. Name's John Ross. Might've worked here a while back."

She squinted at him, then cracked a smile. "Ah. The ginger flash. Mouth on him like a dockhand. Worked for me near two months. Cleaned tables. Broke a bottle on a man's head once— much deserved. Brave fool."

Lewis gripped the bar. "Was he well? Healthy?"

"Aye. Restless though. Always asking questions. Anxious to make more coin, so he worked at another place too, though I can't say where. Said he was looking to join some expedition north. Took up with another lad—well-dressed, English. Name of Nathaniel something. Talked about Delagoa Bay or some place like it. Said they might head up the coast to find some trading post."

Lewis leaned in. "You're sure?"

"Would I lie to a man that pale?" She smiled again, but her tone sobered. "He was a good boy. Gave his bread to a beggar once. I never forgot that."

He left her with a few coins and stepped back into the sun, heart thudding in his chest. Delagoa Bay. It wasn't a certainty—but it was something. And something was better than the silence that had swallowed him since Rockcliffe.

He had direction now. And that, at last, was a beginning.

Lewis's boots clapped the cobbled streets of Cape Town by late morning. The harbor behind him shrank with every step. He moved with a certain looseness now—less stiffness in his bad leg, less fog behind the eyes. This wasn't Rockcliffe. Here he had a purpose.

He skirted past a vegetable cart, then a small group of soldiers on leave, and turned onto a dusty lane that snaked uphill toward the quarter where taverns served both sailors and servants alike. The neighborhood bore little resemblance to the bustling main crag Lewis would've seen years ago, The city had changed in many ways since then. New signs. Different voices.

He asked around, looking for the other place John may have worked.

The third tavern he entered was tucked beneath a corrugated tin awning and shaded by a pair of skinny jacaranda trees. Inside, the air was thick with brewing hops and wood smoke. A Malay man in a threadbare waistcoat was polishing tankards with a frayed cloth behind the bar.

"Lookin' for a boy, I am," Lewis said after ordering a cup of lukewarm tea. "Red hair. Scottish accent. Might've worked here some months back."

The man raised an eyebrow. "Plenty pass through. What kind of boy was this?"

"Lean. Strong for his age. Quick hands and red hair."

"Ah." The barkeep's grin widened. "John something. That's the one. Worked here maybe six weeks. He weren't shy about lettin' folk know he wasn't stayin' long."

Lewis leaned in. "Did he ever mention where he was headed?"

The man shrugged. "Him and that other lad—Nathaniel, they called him. Proper talker, that one. Fancy boots. Said they might join some expedition to… huh. Gone from the head now. Then one day, poof. They disappeared. Like they'd just slipped between the boards."

"Delagoa Bay?" Lewis offered, his heart beginning to pound.

The barkeep snapped his fingers. "That was it! Near enough."

Lewis felt something loosen in his chest—a small knot unraveling. "Remember when?"

"Not really. Been a while."

He stayed a little longer, nursing his cup, asking one or two more questions. But no more clarity came.

Still, it was encouragement. And his heart warmed at the thought that he was in a place where John had been a short time ago.

By late afternoon, Lewis was at the registry office, a squat, whitewashed building with slatted windows and dust-worn floors. He explained his case to a disinterested clerk who fingered a stack of shipping manifests and pointed to a few logs.

Lewis found the entry within minutes. A schooner named *The Mary*. Departed late March. Destination unnamed. No passenger records. But the cargo manifest hinted at trade—cloth, tools, a case of medicinal supplies. Enough to support the theory. And John was always drawn to motion—to movement.

The trail felt warm now.

That night, Lewis returned to the *Annabelle*. He sat near the bow again, the same place he'd stood that morning, but now under a sky full of stars. The breeze carried the scent of the land—smoke and soil and something deeper.

He unfolded Margaret's letter again. The paper was soft now, its edges worn, her handwriting faded but still unmistakable.

"Find him, Lewis," it said. He folded the letter again and pressed it to his chest.

"I'm going, Maggie," he whispered. "I'm going."

By the third day in Cape Town, Lewis's early momentum had ebbed into a frustrating standstill. He paced the harbor, scanning the names of moored vessels, questioning dockhands and traders, and even offering coin for rumors. But few ships were heading up the coast. None were scheduled to Delagoa Bay.

He returned twice to the registry, hoping something new might appear—a sudden merchant journey, a survey expedition, anything. Each time the clerk only shrugged, handed him another stack of manifests, and muttered, "It's the winds. No one favors that route this time of year."

By the sixth day, Lewis stood at the edge of the quay, watching a brig unfurl its sails for Calcutta. His breath came shallow.

Delagoa Bay felt like a promise drifting away with every tide.

That evening, he walked back into the tavern where John had worked. The Malay proprietor gave him a nod of recognition but didn't interrupt his card game. Lewis sat at a corner table, listening to the laughter, the dice clatter, the groan of the city easing into night.

He realized then—he wasn't leaving. Not yet.

The next morning, Lewis set out with a new purpose. He wandered farther inland seeking a modest place to rent a room. A narrow boarding house nestled between a bakery and a wheelwright's shop offered a dim but clean upstairs cot for a few coins a night. The landlady, a sharp-eyed widow named Mrs. Van Heerden, squinted up at him as he stood in the foyer.

"You don't strike me as a man come for leisure."

"I'm not," Lewis said. "Looking for a ship up the coast. Might be here a while."

She pursed her lips and handed him a room key. "No loud drinkers and no tracking in mud."

That afternoon, he asked around for work. A grizzled foreman with a nose like a broken tiller took one look at his missing hand and leg and grunted, "Can you sit still and see straight?"

Lewis nodded.

"Then you'll do. We need someone to watch the cargo sheds at night. Keep a lamp burning and a club ready. Just scare off thieves."

That evening, Lewis took his post beneath the eaves of a warehouse, seated on a stool with a lantern at his feet and a short iron rod across his lap. The harbor sounds kept him company—waves slapping wood, gulls calling, the muffled cries of drunken sailors.

It wasn't noble work. But it was honest.

And it kept him close to the sea.

He would stay in Cape Town until a ship took him closer to the place where he hoped his son still lived. Even if it took weeks. Even if it took longer.

And in the quiet of that night, with Margaret's letter tucked into his coat and the firelight licking the far shed walls, Lewis made peace with waiting.

He wasn't done walking toward his son.

Weeks passed, and Lewis settled into the rhythm of Cape Town's waterfront. During daylight hours, he limped among cargo crates and shadowed canopies, his coat flapping in the salt wind. At night, he watched the harbor like a man expecting an omen. The few ships going up the Natal Coast were not interested in hiring on a man with one arm and one leg.

Among the laborers and merchants he occasionally shared words with, one came to speak with more ease—Johan, a Dutch-born trader with a crooked smile and a deep laugh. They often shared a pipe at dusk, sitting on crates and speaking of weather, shipments, and the misfortunes that chased men across oceans.

One evening, Lewis broached the subject again. "Ever travel north? Toward Delagoa Bay?"

Johan exhaled smoke through his nose and shook his head slowly. "Not if I can help it. That coast..." He gestured vaguely northeast. "It's Zulu country. Fierce men. Shaka's warriors. It's said they can run for days without rest. And they're not fond of white traders on their land."

Lewis stiffened. "But ships still go that way."

"Some. Fewer than before. The risk is high, and the gain's too lean. Most captains avoid the route now unless they've strong escorts."

Johan leaned closer, lowering his voice. "You hear things, working these docks. A caravan of merchants, they say, was surrounded near the Tugela. Spears like lightning, one man said. Another claimed he saw bodies with limbs torn clean off. Wild stories, maybe—but not ones to dismiss. Shaka rules with iron and fire. Even his allies fear him."

Lewis looked away, lips pressed thin.

"You've got someone up there, don't you?" Johan asked quietly.

"My son. Or so I hope."

Johan nodded, his expression sobering. "Then pray he's braver than most."

Lewis turned his gaze back to the water. He could almost see the lad again—barefoot, red-headed, wide-eyed and wily. Brave, yes. But also alone.

The horizon stretched on, empty but waiting.

CHAPTER 18

Days literally melted into each other. The wreck of the *Mary* settled deeper into the sand at low tide, its once-proud lines now little more than the ribs of a carcass. From the cliffs above, gulls wheeled and screamed. Below, the makeshift camp turned desperate. The crew waited, eyes always searching the horizon for a mast, a sail, a flicker of hope. But none came.

Every day began with false hope and ended in exhausted resignation. The men rationed what remained of their supplies. The surgeon, now reduced to boiling leaves for poultices, watched helplessly as fevers took root in several of the crew. Dysentery, swelling bites, festering wounds. The jungle's edge crept closer with each passing hour, as if the land itself wished to reclaim the intruders.

Lieutenant King stood alone one morning, overlooking the strand. His uniform was torn and faded, but he carried himself like a man still in command. A faint line had etched itself deeper each day into the corner of his mouth. He had not slept well in a week. A runner arrived breathless from the inland patrol. No sign of Farewell. No sign of Fynn. No clear trail.

"They were here," said King, scanning the horizon. "But now the land has swallowed them up."

When he turned to face the camp, he saw men unraveling in small ways—one talking to himself as he stirred cold ash, another weeping silently, hunched over a broken musket. One of the porters—the boy with the twisted wrist—had not spoken in days. His eyes were vacant.

King returned to the captain's tent, now a weather-stained canvas sagging on one side. Inside were maps, a compass, three broken field glasses, and the remnants of salt pork.

He called a meeting. The surviving officers and key crew members gathered—Nathaniel, sunburnt and thinner now; the surgeon, whose hands trembled from exhaustion; Liam the Dutchman, ever pragmatic; and John Ross, still ebullient despite the hardships. John had changed, though. There was a new tautness in his frame, a steadiness in his gaze. His feet were blistered but resistant to pain, his red hair bleached even brighter by the sun. He looked like a boy carved out of driftwood and flint.

King gestured to the map splayed across a crate. A red line snaked from their position to an X.

"Delagoa Bay lies here," he said, pointing at the X. "By sea, it would take a few days. But we are not at sea. We are stranded. We have no word from Farewell or Fynn. We have no medicine."

The men nodded grimly.

"The fever will claim more of us if we stay. Food is running low. We are weeks from a proper port without a ship. Nevertheless, I believe someone must reach Delagoa Bay by land."

Murmurs rippled. The surgeon shook his head slowly. "You're suggesting a crossing through the wilderness? That is madness."

"Madness," King replied, evenly, "would be waiting here for a ship that does not come."

Liam cleared his throat. "Even if we made it, we don't know who we'd find. The Portuguese hold the Bay. They might not be willing to help."

"And yet," King said, "it is our only hope."

He looked at each man, his gaze settling finally on John. 'We cannot send a large party. It would draw attention, burn resources, and risk ambush. But one might pass unseen. One with courage. One who already knows how to manage by himself."

John said nothing, but his throat tightened.

Nathaniel spoke first. "You mean John? He's only a boy."

"He's the only one who might succeed," said King.

The silence was deep.

"Give me the map," John said.

Everyone turned.

King unrolled it again. "The journey is nearly four hundred miles. You will need to cross rivers, avoid hostile groups. You'll have a musket, ammunition, a compass, a flint for making fires, and a few days' rations. After that, you forage."

"No shoes," John added.

King blinked. "What?"

"I go barefoot. Boots blister me worse than the trail."

William, who had been standing nearby, stepped forward before the others could respond.

"I go too," he said firmly.

John turned, startled. "William, no—this isn't your burden."

The young man shook his head. "I know the lowland paths. I've spoken with men from the rivers ahead. You do not. Alone, you will waste days or worse."

For a moment, neither of them spoke. The surf hissed behind them, distant and cold.

"I've seen men die from kindness," the ship's surgeon muttered, not looking up from the map he was scrawling on canvas. "Don't let this be one of those times."

William ignored him. His eyes stayed on John. "You came this far with nothing. Let me help you finish."

John searched the man's face, seeing no bravado, only resolve. He nodded slowly. "All right. We walk together."

The next two days were spent in quiet preparation. John sharpened the blade Nathaniel gave him. The porters offered dried maize cakes and advice in low Zulu. One elderly man tied a leather cord around John's wrist for protection.

On the morning of departure, the sky was gray with coastal mist. Nathaniel pressed a hand to John's shoulder. "You're either the bravest lad I've ever met," he said, "or the most foolish."

John grinned faintly. "I suppose we'll both find out."

King studied John's face, then opened the small brass case. The glass face of the compass fogged slightly in the morning chill. "The red needle always points north," he said, steadying the device in his palm. "If you hold it level and turn until north is where you want it, you can follow any direction you please."

John nodded slowly. "And if I get turned around?"

"Then stop, breathe, and start again. The sun rises in the east. Watch the shadows. And don't trust the coastline—rivers bend too much. That map is rough, but it will show you where the main waterways are. Follow them when you can."

John turned the compass over, watching the needle tremble as if uncertain too. "I'll learn it."

King gave him a dry biscuit and a leather pouch with the last of their dried meat. He slung the musket across John's narrow shoulders himself, as if bestowing a ceremonial mantle. "You've got powder and shot enough for a few tries. Don't waste it unless it's life or death."

John nodded again. There was nothing left to say.

When he turned toward the trees, the world seemed impossibly large around him. The heat shimmered off the grass. Insects droned. He took his first steps, bare feet pressing into earth.

Behind him, the crew stood silent. One of the seamen shook his head. "Poor lad won't last two days."

King didn't turn. "Maybe not," he said quietly. "But at least he gives us some hope. So let's imagine him succeeding."

The trees swallowed him whole within minutes. A path—if it could be called that—wound through acacia and thornbush. His bare feet already ached, stabbed by roots, scraped by unseen stones. He paused once, glancing back. The smoke of the wrecked camp still rose faintly in the distance.

He pressed forward into the golden wilds, into a silence so deep it felt ancient. Flies bit at his neck. A strange, clicking bird followed him for an hour. At midday, he crossed a stream—ankle-deep but swift—and sat to drink and cool his feet.

A half-hour later, the sound of the river was behind them, but its coolness lingered in their skin—and something else. John suddenly froze, a look of disgust flashing across his face.

"What is it?" William asked, stepping beside him.

John stumbled backward, slapping at his legs. "Leeches," he said with a gasp. "God, look at them."

Small, glistening creatures clung to his calves and ankles, writhing slowly, bloated with blood. One had burrowed near the back of his knee.

William moved quickly, guiding John to a flat rock and pulling a thin blade from his belt. "Hold still," he said calmly. "If you rip them wrong, the heads stay in."

John clenched his jaw as William scraped carefully, dislodging the leeches one by one. He winced as the last one came free.

"You'll be fine," William said, removing some leeches from his legs as well then rinsing the blade in his canteen and handing John a cloth. "They love slow blood."

John let out a shaky laugh. "Then I must be full of it."

They sat in silence a moment, the heat thick around them, the bush quiet and waiting. Then they rose and pressed on.

He could have turned back. He wasn't yet a full mile from camp. But he remembered the way Lieutenant King had looked at him—not with pity, but with hope. The way Nathaniel had pressed the musket into his hands. The way the surgeon's lips had drawn tight when he spoke of the boys dying under the canvas shelter. The ship's crew had no medicine. No hope. Unless John and William found it.

John stood up, wiped his palms on his trousers, and adjusted the strap of the bag across his shoulder. The jungle ahead looked no kinder than before—but he felt something tighten inside him. A knot of resolve. Let the wilderness come. He was still walking.

And he would keep walking.

CHAPTER 19

The wind came in sharp off the harbor, and Lewis Ross pulled his coat tighter as he limped past the crate stacks. Even with the stump of his leg bound and fitted to the rough peg McDugall had helped carve aboard the *Annabelle*, he moved awkwardly. He had one hand, one leg, and not enough coin to last the month. Cape Town's beauty had dulled quickly in the salt-bitten weeks since he'd arrived. The vibrant city of sails and spices had turned, in his eyes, to stone and shadow.

He felt the slope again.

It began quietly—the old darkness of despair rising through his spine and licking behind his eyes. The cold didn't help. Nor did the endless watching—every night at the docks, every sunrise without word of John. The ships came and went. None to Delagoa Bay. The clerk at the registry no longer looked him in the eye when he handed over another empty manifest sheet.

And then there was the ache.

Not the phantom pain in his missing leg, but the ache of time—that gnawing erosion that sanded down the edges of hope. Lewis had seen it before, in his own father's eyes, long after his mother had died. That hollow certainty that time would win.

He found himself standing outside a tavern door one evening, staring at the swing of it as sailors passed in and out. The scent of yeast and whisky curled into the street. A laugh broke inside. He imagined himself through the door, cup in hand, forgetting.

Johan found him there.

"Go in, and you'll come out a beggar," the Dutchman said, appearing beside him. "Or you won't come out at all."

Lewis looked at him sideways. "Smells better than salt and sweat."

Johan shrugged. "Aye. So did the Devil's breath the first time I kissed it. Two years I lost to drink. Woke up naked in a Port Elizabeth alley with blood on my knuckles and no clue whose."

Lewis snorted. "You always this gentle?"

"No. But I know the look of a man pressed against the door of ruin."

Lewis didn't move. The wind cut again.

"Come on," Johan said. "Got lentils and something like meat."

They walked back toward the boarding house. That night, Lewis didn't drink. But he did stare at the ceiling so long he began to see constellations in the water stains.

A week later, Lewis stood again on the quay, squinting at a modest schooner moored beside a sugar barge. Her name—*Maria Louisa*—was painted in chipped gold along the side. She was lean, modest, and rough-looking, but her deck was tidy and the crew wasn't drunk.

Johan had told him this ship might be different.

"She's not afraid of the coast," he had said. "Not many left who aren't. The captain's stubborn and careful. Rare mix."

And so Lewis waited, cane in hand, watching for the man who ran the ship.

When the captain emerged—tall, dark-skinned, with a wool cap pulled low and a ledger under his arm—Lewis approached. "You're Captain Tembo?"

"I am." The man's voice was measured and cool.

"I'm looking for passage to Delagoa Bay."

Tembo paused. His eyes dropped to Lewis's leg. Then to his missing hand.

"This isn't a passenger vessel."

"I don't have coin for passage. Not asking for leisure. I'm asking to earn my keep."

"What could you do, friend?"

Lewis bristled but kept his voice steady. "I can watch. I can listen. I've stood guard over goods for two months without losing so much as a hinge. I worked the Annabelle under Captain McDugall all the way from Scotland to here. I don't eat much. And I don't complain."

"McDugall's a good man, but you have one leg missing."

"And still stand longer than men with two. Try me."

Tembo looked over his shoulder, then motioned Lewis toward the edge of the dock. "Come with me."

They stepped aboard the *Maria Louisa*. The deck swayed gently beneath them. Tembo called over a wiry young mate and spoke low. The mate nodded, pointed Lewis toward the hold.

"I need someone who can read the stars. Can you do that?"

"No."

"Do you cook?"

"No."

"Can you repair canvas?"

"I patched sails on the Annabelle," Lewis said quietly. "Stitched them with one hand and teeth. Slower than most, but I did it."

Tembo raised a brow.

"I can keep watch." Lewis added. "I can stand guard while your crew sleeps. I'll haul what I can, eat what I'm given, sleep where there's space. Just give me north."

Tembo was quiet for a long time.

"You a soldier once?"

"I was."

"You ever sail?"

"For years, before a shark took my leg."

The captain turned, walked the lthe deck and came back. "We leave on the spring tide. We call at Port Natal, then north. You pull your weight or I put you ashore."

Lewis felt the weight of weeks break off his back.

"I'll be ready."

Tembo nodded once. "Bring your own gear. And a sober stomach."

That evening, Lewis sat with Johan beneath the same lamplight they'd shared for weeks.

"He said yes," Lewis muttered, still stunned.

Johan chuckled. "Told you he was strange."

"But I'm afraid."

"Of dying?"

"Of finding nothing. Or worse."

Johan nodded slowly. "I once chased my brother all the way to Zanzibar. Took six months. When I got there, he was already gone. Left behind a ring and a lie."

Lewis said nothing.

"But I was glad I went," Johan continued. "Because after that, I could live forward."

Lewis looked out at the stars. "I think I've been living backward too long."

Johan smiled. "Then go north, watchman. Even ghosts need wind at their back."

The days passed quickly. Lewis gathered what gear he could—sparse clothes, a knife, oilskin wrap, rope, Margaret's letter, and the makeshift compass he'd bought. Every item was chosen with care. He cleaned the stump, polished the peg leg, even let Mrs. Van Heerden braid the coat sleeve +for his missing arm so the flapping wouldn't annoy the crew.

On the last night before departure, he returned to the tavern where John had once worked. It was quiet. A new boy—no older than John had been—was scrubbing the floor.

Lewis drank tea. Nothing stronger.

When he rose to leave, he pressed a coin into the boy's palm. "If anyone ever asks after a lad named John Ross—red hair, Scottish tongue—you tell them his da went north."

The boy nodded, wide-eyed.

Outside, the night air smelled of brine and change.

Lewis turned north.

At last.

CHAPTER 20

The morning haze hung low over the land like breath caught between exhale and prayer. A soft wind stirred the tall grass, bending it in sweeping arcs that shimmered silver under the light of a pale sun.

John paused at the edge of the slope and looked back. The ocean was gone now, lost behind the folds of distant hills, and with it the wreck of the *Mary*. Before him stretched an endless, undulating veldt—alive with sound, shadow and heat.

William stepped up beside him, his eyes scanning the horizon. "You see that tree line?" he said, pointing. "That's mopane. Good shade there. We'll make it by noon if we keep a steady pace."

John nodded and adjusted the strap of his pack. His musket, wrapped in oilcloth, rested across his back. The air was already warming, thick with the scents of dust and dry vegetation. Insects whirred unseen. Somewhere to the east, a bird let out a high, looping cry.

They descended slowly, boots crunching against loose shale and sun-baked earth. The trail, such as it was, wound past termite mounds and low-thorn scrub. Occasionally, William would stoop to point out animal tracks—springbok, jackal, once even a lion.

"How do you know it's a lion?" John asked.

William crouched beside the print. "See how wide it is? And the pad marks—too large for any dog. Also, no claws. Cats keep theirs pulled in when they walk." He smiled slightly. "We won't see it, not unless it wants us to."

John didn't find that particularly reassuring.

The land changed with every mile. What began as open grassland gave way to rockier ridges, where scrubby acacia trees offered meager shade. In a shallow ravine, they found a narrow stream and refilled their water gourds. William moved deftly, scanning the ground for signs of snakes or scorpions before kneeling.

"Drink here," he said. "Fast-moving. Less likely to carry sickness."

John crouched beside him, splashing water on his face before taking a long, grateful gulp. The heat pressed close, not yet unbearable, but building.

They moved in silence for a while, each man lost in his own rhythm. John thought of the others—of Nathaniel, left behind; of the crew and the burning ribs of the ship; of his mum, growing ever fainter in his memory but still the reason for his forward steps.

By late morning they reached the mopane grove, its papery leaves fluttering in the dry wind. They rested in the shade, chewing on dried biltong and hard biscuits.

William retrieved a small tin of salt from his pouch and sprinkled some into his water. "Keeps your body strong when you sweat," he explained.

John copied him, then leaned back against a tree trunk and exhaled. "Feels like another world already."

William looked at him, his gaze steady. "It is. Every mile from the sea is a mile closer to the places that maps forget."

A sound caught their ears then—low voices, the clatter of hooves. William motioned quickly for John to remain still, then crept forward to the edge of the trees.

A small party of men was moving along a distant ridge accompanied by a pair of oxen. They were lean and dark-skinned, dressed in skins and carrying short spears and knobkerries.

William returned with a nod. "Not Zulu. Not yet, anyway. Come. We greet them."

John followed, wary but curious. As they approached, William raised a hand in greeting and called out a few phrases in a language John did not recognize. One of the tribesmen responded cautiously, then stepped forward. An exchange followed—quick, musical, full of subtle gestures.

Later, as the men shared a gourd of thick, fermented milk, William leaned toward John and said quietly, "They are Sotho, from a village not far. They warn us to keep east—Zulu raiders seen not two weeks past. Burned a homestead. Took cattle."

John swallowed hard. "Do Sotho fight Zulu?"

William shook his head. "No. They run. Fight and you die. That's what they believe."

They camped that night not far from the Sotho, close enough to feel less alone but distant enough to respect boundaries. John lay under the stars, listening to the soft rattle of insects and the distant murmur of tribal singing. William had rolled a thin blanket around his shoulders and was humming to himself, the wooden beads at his neck catching stray firelight.

"You've traveled this way before?" John asked softly.

"Not all the way. Not yet."

"But you know what's coming."

William was silent for a while. Then he said, "I know stories. I know fear. We'll need more than musket balls to enter their land."

By the fifth day, the last of the hardtack was gone. They chewed on strips of salted beef until even that turned to brittle threads.

John rationed each remaining shot for the musket, choosing targets only when they offered clear, still silhouettes—small antelope or guinea fowl, never more than one at a time. A single bird meant a hot meal. A missed shot meant hunger.

One morning, after a dawn mist gave way to a punishing sun, William spotted a cluster of plump, glossy fruit high in a tree. He climbed like a lizard, legs wrapped around the trunk, fingers finding cracks in the bark. When he came down, he held a pouch of small green pods.

"Wild tamarind," he said. "Good for strength. But too many makes gut twist."

They ate a few. John's stomach grumbled but accepted them. By nightfall, he felt hollow again.

The land itself resisted entry. Streams they hoped would hold fish proved shallow or scummed over. Birds called from hidden places but vanished when approached.

Once, William pulled a tiny white mushroom from under a stump and sniffed it. "Death cap," he said. "Looks like food. Isn't."

John tried not to stare at the ration pouch, now near-empty. That night, he caught himself counting the musket balls by touch, a litany of dwindling hope.

Still, William made things stretch. He showed John how to dig for edible roots in dry riverbeds, how to tie reeds into loops for snaring, how to sip water from moss without disturbing the nest of ants nearby.

John listened, watched, copied. It reminded him of when he'd first learned to gut fish as a boy—when every survival trick had felt like a treasure.

One afternoon, while following a game trail along a cracked ridgeline, John spotted movement ahead. He dropped to one knee, cocked the musket, waited.

A duiker—a small antelope—picked its way through the underbrush, head lowered.

John exhaled slowly and fired.

The musket roared.

The duiker dropped.

They skinned and cleaned it quickly beneath a wind-shifted sky, smoke rising soon after from a ring of stones. The meat was lean but rich. They ate with quiet thanks.

That night, the air changed again. Clouds massed in the distance, black and rolling like smoke from a ruined town.

"Rain," William said. "Maybe storm."

John looked at the meat still hanging to dry.

They both began tying what they could into oilskins and canvas. Storm or not, they had food for two days. But few shots left.

The journey pressed on.

The days grew longer, and the landscape leaned toward the surreal. Baobab trees loomed like petrified giants. The grasses reached shoulder-high in some glades. In others, fire-scorched earth smoked quietly beneath their feet. Here and there, they passed broken kraals—abandoned villages with toppled fences and fire-pocked huts, the signs of flight and fear. Insects buzzed thick and loud. At times, the air itself felt restless, like it remembered something terrible.

By the fifth day, the river they'd loosely followed curved eastward, cutting away from their intended path. William judged that if they continued to hug its banks, they'd lose precious time.

"We head inland tomorrow," he said, crouched over a map drawn from memory, tracing lines in the dirt. "Cut across the hills. The high veldt will be dry, but we'll make speed."

John nodded, rubbing the back of his neck. "You're sure?"

William gave a half-smile. "No. But I trust my feet more than the water. And the Zulu don't linger in those hills. Bad spirits, they say."

That night they camped beneath an umbrella thorn tree, where the stars tangled in its flat canopy and the wind carried the screeches of night creatures they couldn't name. The fire was small and quiet. John laid out his powder horn and musket balls, counting slowly.

"Six left," he said.

"Only use if needed. We can trap, if the land offers."

But the land was stingier now. Dry roots, sour berries, the occasional hare if they were lucky. One morning, William caught a fat tortoise and roasted it whole. It helped. But it wasn't enough.

They pressed on, stomachs tightening with each passing day. John felt it in his shoulders, his legs—the way the horizon seemed farther than before, not because the land had changed, but because he had. They moved quieter, spoke less. Hunger taught its own kind of silence.

Then came the snake.

John had stepped into a patch of warm sand near a kopje when he felt the flick of motion near his ankle. Instinct yanked him backward just as the puff adder struck. Its fangs missed by inches, but the hiss it left in the air sounded like anger incarnate.

William dropped his bundle and drew his knife in a single motion. The blade flashed. The snake coiled again, ready to strike. But William was faster. He pinned it behind the head with a forked stick and slashed cleanly, severing the head with precision.

They both stood panting.

"Did it bite?" William asked, his voice hard.

John checked, shaking his head. "Close. Damn close."

William crouched over the carcass. "Puff adder. Quiet killer. Slow, but no warning." He glanced up, eyes serious. "If it had struck... we would not have reached help."

John exhaled and sat on a flat stone, heart thudding. "Thanks."

They skinned and cooked the snake. Its meat was chewy but filling. The crisis shook something loose in both of them. That night, they talked longer than they had in days—about the wind near the coast, the heat, the ships they'd known, the differences between their homes. They didn't speak of death, though it had squatted beside them like a third traveler.

They rose the next morning before the sun crested the thorn trees, both men leaner than they had been when they left the wreck. William's cheekbones had sharpened, and John's shirt hung looser around his shoulders, the fabric damp with salt and sweat. Their legs ached with every step, but they pressed inland, away from the snake-haunted kopjes and toward higher, drier ground.

By midday, the terrain shifted again—gentler slopes gave way to rolling flats of pale grass that stretched in golden waves toward the low escarpments in the distance. A lone herd of eland stirred in the heat shimmer and galloped off as they crested a rise.

"I know this ridge," William said quietly, his voice dry with fatigue. "There's a village two days east. Maybe less."

John nodded. He could feel it too. Something changing—not just in the land, but in themselves. They were no longer just surviving. They were advancing. Still thin, still sore, but determined.

That evening, they made camp in a sunken gully that cradled a trickling spring. It wasn't much, but it was cold and sweet, and they drank until their bellies cramped. The fire they built was the largest they dared light in days.

They sat beside it, watching the smoke rise in ghostly tendrils.

"Tell me something," John said after a long silence. "Why do you really want to go back north? If you were smart, you'd have stayed with the others, waited for another ship."

William stirred the coals with a stick. "Smart men wait. That's why they die forgotten. The ones who live longest are the ones who walk—even when the path burns."

John looked into the flames. "You've seen it, haven't you? The worst of it."

William's jaw tensed. "Enough to know the Zulu aren't just warriors. They're a storm. They move like water. Like wind through bone. One day you hear a story, the next your village is gone. Not just burned. Gone."

John thought of the abandoned kraals, the empty huts, the children with wary eyes. "Why do you keep going, then?"

William's gaze didn't waver. "Because the land is bigger than fear. And because I owe people. And maybe..." He paused, voice quieter. "Maybe I want to see what kind of man you'll be when we get there."

The fire popped softly. A pair of jackals yipped in the distance.

John reached into his satchel and pulled out the final biscuit from their rations. He split it in half and handed one piece to William. "Then we keep going."

They left again before dawn. The moon still hung low in the west, casting long shadows as they climbed the rise and looked toward the dark line of forest far ahead. Somewhere beyond it lay the next village, perhaps even a patrol or an outpost—someone who could carry word of the wreck, someone who might help.

Their boots slapped dry earth. Their shadows stretched forward.

By late morning, John spotted thin smoke on the horizon, not the curling kind of a cooking fire, but the wide smudge of settlement. He pointed, breath catching. "There," he said.

William shielded his eyes. "Let's hope it's friendly."

They didn't speak much as they descended toward it—just the sound of grass crunching beneath their boots and the slow, steady thump of blood in their ears. John's musket was slung low but ready. William's knife was at his side.

Still walking. Still rising.

Still alive.

CHAPTER 21

Morning broke pale and windless. A thin mist clung to the lower slopes of the hills, rising like breath from the earth itself. John Ross stood on a granite outcrop, scanning the terrain below. They had entered gentler country now—undulating hills blanketed with golden grass interspersed with patches of thornbush and groves of wild fig. It was not empty land. Faint traces of footpaths braided the slopes, and distant smudges of smoke marked the presence of people.

William joined him, wiping dew from his face with a dark blue cloth. "We're close," he said. "People live in this valley. Mpondo, I think. My mother's mother was one of them."

John adjusted the musket slung over his shoulder. "Friendly?"

William gave a slow nod. "If we come open-handed. They don't like the Zulu. Or the Ndwandwe. We'll be safer here than deeper west."

That word, Ndwandwe, was new to John. He glanced at his companion, eyebrows raised.

William caught the look and elaborated. "The Ndwandwe are another power. Strong as the Zulu, maybe more clever. They've been raiding north and east. Big battle coming, they say. Whole valleys will bleed before it ends."

John said nothing, but the air between them grew heavier with the notion of a war between giants. And they were walking toward it.

They descended the slope cautiously, sticking to the animal trails and pausing often to listen. Birds flitted through the acacia branches. A hare bounded from its hiding place, nearly brushing John's boot. The stillness had weight to it—a hush that felt less like peace and more like waiting.

By midday, they crested a ridge and saw the village below.

It sat in a fold of the hills protected by natural rises and a thorn-stocked barrier wall. Mud-brick huts with high thatched roofs formed a loose ring around a central kraal. A few figures moved slowly among the enclosures. Smoke drifted from cookfires, and goats bleated near the outer fence. But it was not the busy bustle of Cape Town or the soundscape of Port Natal. Here, life moved to an older and slower rhythm.

"We wait," William said, holding out an arm to stop John. "Let them see us first. If they want to talk, they will."

John nodded and crouched beside him, hidden partially by a low screen of brush. He took the chance to drink from the water gourd.

They waited fifteen minutes, maybe longer, before a figure emerged from the village and began walking toward them. The man was tall and bare-chested, his skin the deep bronze of sun-hardened years. He wore a beaded necklace and carried a short spear in one hand and a round shield in the other. No war paint. No companions.

"Good," William said. "That's a talker, not a fighter."

John remained still as William stood, hands spread wide. He called out something—sharp syllables, unfamiliar to John's ears, but confident. The stranger replied, not slowing his pace. As he drew nearer, John could see that he was not young, perhaps in his forties, with the long scars of a healed wound crossing his left shoulder.

The two men exchanged words in a rapid tongue John did not understand. Then William turned slightly.

"He says we're welcome, but we must hand over our weapons at the gate. Custom."

John hesitated.

"He says we'll get them back when we go," William added. "And if we don't go, they'll just watch us starve. It's that kind of land."

John unslung the musket, unstrapped the powder horn, and handed both to William. "Tell him we mean no harm."

William translated, and the man nodded once, serious but not unfriendly. They walked the rest of the way together.

The Mpondo village sat in a natural hollow between two ridges, its huts arranged in a wide circle, smoke rising from their thatched tops like breath from a sleeping animal. At the center was a broad communal hearth and a tall, carved post painted with ochre and charcoal—an ancestral marker. William whispered that it was likely for the spirits of those killed in raids.

When the two boys arrived, they were watched warily at first. But William, with patience and a practiced smile, spoke a dialect that bridged his own tongue and theirs. He explained they were peaceful travelers headed north and avoiding the larger trails It helped that both of them looked half-starved and harmless.

An old woman with a spine curved like a bow came forward and placed a hand on John's shoulder. Her fingers were like claws, warm and trembling. She muttered something, and William translated: "She says we are marked with dust and far walking. That we smell of rivers and bone."

John glanced at him. "Is that good?"

William gave a tight-lipped smile. "Better than if she said we smelled like warriors."

They were allowed to sit by the outer fires. The meal was thin maize porridge, not much, but offered freely. Children stared at John's musket, eyes wide. William, ever cautious, rested his hand over the pouch that held the last of the ammunition. That night, they slept beside the chicken coops under a woven mat the size of a blanket.

In the morning, a younger man—bare-chested with a spear slung over his back—approached as they packed their things.

"You're heading into bad country," he said in slow, accented words. "The Zulu hunt up there. And worse, the Ndwandwe have been moving again. There was fighting near the Mbizana river three nights ago. People speak of drums like thunder and warriors who vanish like smoke."

William listened carefully. "The Zulu and Ndwandwe are both near?"

The man nodded. "They clash often now. The Zulu send scouts even this far south to test the edges."

He paused, then added in a lower voice, "When the great war comes—and it will—we will all be drawn in. There is no more away from it."

John felt a tightening in his gut. This was not just danger. It was history unfolding, like cracks in the earth before a quake. He glanced at William, who was silent, eyes narrowed—not afraid, exactly, but alert in a way John had come to understand meant trouble.

Before they left, the old woman from the previous night handed them a leather pouch filled with dried root. "She says it keeps fever down," William said, pocketing it.

"And if it doesn't?"

"Then it at least keeps the spirits busy trying."

They walked north again that day, through high veldt and narrow forest paths where the wind carried strange smells—ash, wild honey, distant fire. The signs of battle were scattered and quiet—an abandoned spear haft, a bloodied rag tangled in thorn, vultures circling over distant scrub.

For the first time, John realized they were moving through a land not only unfamiliar, but unraveling.

The trail narrowed as they climbed a ridge pocked with boulders. Lichen crusted the stone, and in some places, the path dissolved into little more than dry dust and grass. William led now, his feet quick and sure, pausing often to listen—not to any specific sound, but to the absence of birds or the sharp shift in wind.

"Still smells like old smoke," John muttered behind him, wiping his brow. "But I don't see any fire."

"Old doesn't mean dead," William said without turning. "When Zulu warriors burn a place, the land remembers. And the land never dies."

They crested the ridge near midday. Below them lay a shallow valley, and in its center, a charred smear of what had once been a kraal. Even from a distance, John could see bones—animal, maybe human—white against the blackened earth.

They did not go down. They circled wide.

As they descended into a shaded hollow, a flock of startled guinea fowl burst from the underbrush. John raised his musket, but William stopped him with a hand. "Too noisy," he whispered "If anyone's watching, they'd hear the shot from miles off."

John lowered the weapon. He was getting better at reading William's instincts, even when they disagreed with his own. That was new for him—following, not leading.

That night, they camped beneath a fig tree whose roots spilled like fingers down a slope. William roasted a lizard over a small flame, humming quietly some old tune that John didn't know but felt in his chest. He'd become thinner since they'd left the Mary. His shoulders looked bonier, but his eyes remained sharp.

"You think that kraal was Zulu work?" John asked.

William shook his head. "Could be. But it smelled wrong."

"Smelled wrong?"

"Zulu raid fast. Loud. Then gone. But that place—they were punished. Made an example of. That's not how Shaka fights. Not usually."

"Then who?"

William's face darkened. "Could be Ndwandwe. Or even deserters. Some men just burn because they can."

John stared into the fire. "There's not much left out here, is there?"

"Not much that stays standing."

The next day, they found a trail of prints in the soft riverbank earth. Too many to count. Some barefoot, some with broken sandals. All headed west. The tracks were shallow but fresh—only a day old, maybe less.

"They're moving fast," William said. "But not warriors. Too disorganized."

"Fleeing something?"

"Or following."

They moved carefully after that, avoiding open ground. Twice they heard voices—distant, echoing from unseen paths—but saw no one. The land pressed in with thicker bush, fewer birds, heat rising even before midday. Rations were running low again.

That night, while John scraped together kindling, William stood at the edge of the clearing, staring west.

"There's something else," he said quietly. "Old people say the ground here is cursed."

John laughed, tired and sore. "Everything's cursed out here."

"No," William said. "This place especially. There was a battle here long ago. A bad one. Not the kind you write songs about. The kind you bury and forget."

John looked toward the trees but saw nothing. The sky above them was purple and streaked with ash-colored clouds.

"How do you know?" he asked.

William crouched and ran his fingers through the dust. "The land tells you. You just have to listen."

And in the silence that followed, even John began to hear it— the hush, the waiting, the breath the earth seemed to hold.

They caught sight of the smoke before they saw the settlement. It curled upward in a thin, steady line, pale gray against the afternoon sky. Not the wild plumes of a burning village, nor the intermittent puffs of a traveler's fire—but the calm, sustained breath of cooking fires, of daily life persisting in a land growing more dangerous by the week.

William signaled for John to stay low. They moved into a crouch and crept along the scrub-choked edge of the slope. From behind a stand of sickle bush, they saw them—a cluster of thatched huts laid out in a semi-circle around an open kraal fenced with thick branches. Women moved between them with baskets and jars. A few children chased each other near the animal pens. Several men, bare-chested and broad-shouldered, stood talking near the edge of the compound, spears propped against their thighs.

William exhaled. "Mpondo."

"Mpondo?" John echoed, barely above a whisper.

William nodded. "They live closer to the coast, but some have been pushed inland. Refugees, maybe. Could be they fled the fighting."

He stepped out from the bush without fear, shoulders relaxed. John followed a moment later, unsure but trusting.

As they approached, a pair of armed men intercepted them. William raised both hands and said something in a language John didn't recognize—clicks and rolling vowels. The guards listened, glancing at one another, then lowered their spears slightly. One of them gestured toward the kraal.

An older man awaited them there. He was wrapped in a heavy red-and-black blanket despite the heat. His beard was streaked with gray, but his eyes burned with clarity. William bowed his head. John followed suit.

"They call him Maqoma," William explained quietly as they were led to sit on low stools. "A name of honor. He's not a king—but a man others listen to."

The conversation unfolded in the rhythmic cadence of isiXhosa tinged with dialects John couldn't follow. He caught his own name once, and the word *Shaka* more than once. William spoke fluidly, gesturing occasionally toward the horizon, the river, even the musket John carried. At last, Maqoma replied, short and firm, and William turned to John.

"He says you carry the white man's thunder stick—but you walk like someone who has buried more than he's hunted."

John blinked. "What does that mean?"

William grinned faintly. "I think he means you look tired."

They were offered roasted yams and sour milk, which John took gratefully. After they ate, the mood shifted. The older man leaned in, speaking with a low, steady voice that made William sit straighter.

When William translated, his tone was serious. "He says the Zulu and the Ndwandwe are circling each other like hawks. Shaka sends out impis—regiments—to raid and test defenses. The Ndwandwe answer with ambushes. Every village caught in between gets swept up in it or destroyed."

John frowned. "So... it's war?"

"Not yet," William said. "But close. The Mpondo here say they've seen the signs. War smoke on three horizons. Goat herds driven into hiding. Scouts taken in the night. Children having dreams they don't speak of."

John felt the weight of it in his stomach, the creeping inevitability.

Maqoma spoke again, softer now, his gaze fixed on William.

"He says we should not go west," William translated slowly. "He says death follows the river there. A path of vultures."

John looked toward the setting sun. "But the mission... the men... They could be cut there."

William nodded. "I told him that. He said only this: 'Then let your spirits walk lightly, and your footprints fade behind you.'"

They slept that night in a hut with reed mats and a roof that groaned when the wind shifted. The scent of firewood clung to everything. Outside, a child cried once and was hushed.

John lay awake for a long time listening to the wind, thinking of the path ahead—of what kind of death might follow rivers, and whether they would know it when it came.

CHAPTER 22

The *Maria Louisa* sliced northward along the Natal coast, her sails taut against the evening sky. The breeze was fair, the water slack and glinting like stretched glass. Lewis Ross sat alone near the forward mast, his good hand rough with tar and rope burn, watching the shoreline slip by like a dream he could almost touch.

He hadn't spoken much to the others. He was stronger now, steadier on his feet, but words still caught in his throat, as if sobriety had stripped his tongue bare. The crew didn't ask questions, and Lewis didn't volunteer answers. He was just another member of the crew, quiet and capable. They let him be.

Until the third night, that is, when the wind fell and the ship settled into the slow rock of calm waters, and one of the younger deckhands—Tom Duffy, he called himself—sidled up with a tin mug and a too-easy grin.

"Quiet out here, aye?" Tom said, lowering himself beside Lewis. "You've the look of a man listening to ghosts. Some of 'em tied to the loss of limbs, I expect."

Lewis gave a grunt that could've been agreement. The sea, after all, was full of ghosts.

Tom nudged the mug toward him. "Coffee. Or near enough. You look like you could use it."

Lewis took the drink, grateful more for the gesture than the contents. "Thanks."

Tom didn't speak again right away. Just sat, the two of them breathing in the hush of a cloudless night.

Eventually, Lewis asked, "You ever have a boy?"

Tom blinked. "Me? Nah. Too young, too smart to have an offspring. Why?"

Lewis hesitated, then said, "I lost mine. Or maybe he lost me. Not sure there's a difference anymore."

Tom glanced sideways, brows raised—but he didn't laugh or shrug it off. "You looking for him?"

Lewis nodded slowly. "He ran. Or sailed, I think. South Africa. I... I was drunk when he left. Might've been drunk his whole life, truth be told."

Tom leaned forward, elbows on knees. "That why you're out here now? To find him?"

Lewis gave a small, bitter smile. "Tryin'. Not sure what I'll say if I do."

For a long moment, the only sound was the creak of the rigging and the hush of the sea licking the hull. Then Tom said, "Takes a kind of courage, that. Admitting you were the bastard in the story."

Lewis looked at him, startled.

"I mean it," Tom said. "Most men'd twist it around. Blame the boy. Say he was ungrateful, wild. But you—you're owning it."

Lewis shook his head. "Doesn't make me good. Just tired of lying to myself."

Tom chuckled. "Tiredness is a start."

They sat in silence again. A gull cried somewhere behind them. Lewis leaned his head back and let the stars come into view, sharp as arrowheads. He hadn't felt this kind of quiet in years—not the stillness of drink, but a quiet earned.

"You ever wish you could go back?" Tom asked, voice softer.

"Every day."

Tom nodded. "Well, maybe you don't need to. Maybe going forward's enough."

Lewis turned toward him. In the lamplight, Tom's face looked young—too young to speak like this. But sincere.

"Thanks," Lewis said.

Tom tapped his mug to Lewis's and stood. "Get some sleep. Tomorrow's a long haul."

Lewis stayed seated long after Tom left, staring at the shoreline, whispering prayers he didn't believe in. He hadn't meant to say so much. But it had come out like a confession to salt and stars. And for once, it hadn't burned.

On the next day, the schooner rocked under a low, slate sky as dusk crept in from the east. The wind had shifted all afternoon, unpredictable and teasing, and the mate had begun barking corrections every few minutes. But down on the deck near the coiled hawser and spare sailcloth, Lewis sat with his back against the railing, legs drawn up, watching the sea darken.

Tom was beside him again. The younger man had proven himself nimble and quick-mouthed, easily liked by the crew, though something restless shimmered beneath his friendliness. He'd sought Lewis out during quiet moments, asking him about Scotland, about farming, about the highlands.

Tonight, Tom spoke softly, his voice nearly lost beneath the slosh of the sea. "You ever make peace with him?"

Lewis didn't answer right away. The question caught him off guard. "With who?"

"Your boy," Tom said. "The one you're chasing halfway across the world."

Lewis sighed. "Not much peace to be had. He ran. I didn't stop him. And there's things I did… words I can't take back."

Tom was quiet for a moment, then said, "My father used to take a whip to me. Leather belt, mostly. Sometimes a fire poker. Said it was God's will. Said I was born wicked."

Lewis looked over, startled.

Tom's face was hard in profile, mouth flat. "I ran at thirteen. Hid in a wagon and never looked back. Sometimes I think I should have turned around. Maybe stood up to him. But I was too small. Too scared."

Lewis didn't know what to say. The silence between them was weighted with old bruises.

After a while, Lewis said, "I wasn't like that."

"No?" Tom's voice had sharpened. "So what were you? Just drunk? Too busy? Or did you just not care?"

The change in tone stung. Lewis blinked. "What?"

"You talk about the boy like he's a ghost you can't catch. But I've seen this before, Mr. Ross. A man runs from what he's done, then makes a whole story out of it so he doesn't have to face what he is."

Lewis sat forward. "You don't know me."

"No, I don't," Tom said coldly. "But I know what it feels like to wait at the door and hope someone loves you enough to change. And when they don't—when they never do—that carves something out of you."

Other sailors had drifted near, drawn by Tom's raised voice. A few cast glances at Lewis. Tom stood and dusted off his hands.

"You want my advice?" he said bitterly. "Stop chasing him. You're not the kind of father he needs."

Tom walked off, leaving Lewis surrounded by the eyes of men who had overheard enough to guess the shape of the conversation. The shame came like a second tide—low, cold, and merciless. Lewis pressed his fingers to his brow, wishing he could vanish into the darkening sea.

But in that moment, he felt something else too. Not just shame. *Anger.* Not at his son. At himself, yes. But also at Tom—for baiting him, for tearing the wound wider under the guise of sympathy. And yet... hadn't he deserved it?

He sat long after the others had moved on, staring out over the black horizon, wondering what kind of man he truly was—and whether it mattered if he could be someone better now.

The wind shifted again after midnight. At first it was just a tremble in the rigging, a moaning higher than the usual creak of the masts. Then the canvas began to flap, and a great wall of black loomed to the southeast where the moon should have been.

"Squall!" came the call from the forward watch.

Men spilled from below deck in their shirts and bare feet, scrambling to shorten sail. The mate bellowed orders that were lost to the rising roar. And the sea, once choppy, now heaved like a thing alive.

Lewis had been half-dozing in the galley nook when the storm broke. He stumbled up to the deck as the first sheets of rain slammed across the schooner, cold and horizontal. The lanterns were already out. Lightning flared—blue-white veins streaking the sky—and in the flash, he saw the mainsail twist like a broken wing, then tear

The boom slammed across the deck with terrifying force. Someone screamed. Another flash—a man was down near the railing, blood on his shirt, crew swarming toward him. Then darkness again, wind howling louder.

The schooner groaned as it listed, ropes flailing, wood shrieking. Lewis fought to stay upright. A heavy wave broke over the starboard bow, sweeping two men from their feet—and one of them, he realized with a jolt, was Tom.

The young sailor was flailing at the rail, half overboard, one hand clinging to the broken netting. His eyes met Lewis's for a split second—wild, terrified—and the sea surged again.

Lewis didn't think. He was moving before the next wave hit.

He slammed into the railing and grabbed Tom's wrist with his one good hand. Salt and rain blinded him. Tom's weight dragged him forward. And without a second hand, Lewis had to wrangle his leg and foot into the netting to keep from being pulled into the sea. Lewis shouted, gritted his teeth, and pulled with everything he had. For one awful moment, he thought he would go over too.

Then—help. Two more crewmen grabbed his shoulders and heaved. Tom collapsed onto the deck, coughing seawater and clutching his ribs. Lewis fell beside him, breathless, body trembling.

The squall raged on. But for a moment, Lewis heard only his heartbeat.

Later, after the worst had passed and the mainsail was lashed down and the injured seen to, Lewis found Tom again, wrapped in a blanket near the galley stove. He was pale and shivering, but conscious.

Their eyes met. Tom tried to speak, but Lewis held up a hand. "Don't," he said. "Just don't."

Tom swallowed and looked away. Whatever he'd been about to say, it died in his mouth.

Lewis turned and stepped back into the night. The deck was slick with rain and blood and broken rope. The sea had quieted, but his hand still shook.

He didn't feel proud. He didn't feel forgiven. But something had shifted. Not in Tom but in himself.

He hadn't hesitated. And in that one act, he'd proven—to someone, maybe only to himself—that the man he used to be wasn't the one he had to remain.

The dawn came meek and gray, the sea tamed into slow, guilty swells. The schooner limped forward under a patched sail, rigging frayed and spirits low. The mate's voice was hoarse from shouting through the storm, and the cook doled out hardtack with a silent nod, as if mourning the quiet.

Lewis sat on a crate by the quarterdeck, his crutch leaning beside him, his coat stiff with salt. The knot behind his ribs ached with every breath, but he welcomed it. It reminded him he was alive.

Tom shuffled toward him slowly. His lip was split and one cheek bore the bruise of a swinging block. A blanket clung to his shoulders like penance.

He stood a few paces away. "You should've let me go."

Lewis didn't look up. "Didn't."

Tom hesitated, then eased himself onto the deck, cross-legged like a penitent. He rubbed at the back of his neck. "I was wrong. About what I said. About what I told the others."

Lewis's jaw clenched. "They already thought it."

"I made it worse," Tom said. "I was angry. Not at you. At the story. Your son... your guilt. I didn't know what to do with it. Felt like someone dropped a mirror in front of me, and I didn't like what I saw."

Lewis turned his face slightly, enough to glance at the young man. "You said something about your own father."

Tom nodded. "He used to tell me I was his punishment. He wouldn't even look at me after I turned ten. Hit me sometimes, but mostly ignored me. I left home at twelve. The sea was the first thing that didn't turn away."

There was silence but for the wheeze of the wind and the occasional clatter of a loose cleat.

Lewis said, "You still chose to hurt someone else."

"I did," Tom said softly. "I do that when I get scared. When I think someone might see too much."

Lewis shifted his weight, the roughly carved wooden peg creaking against the stump. "You said I should've let you go. But I didn't. You think I did that for you?"

Tom blinked. "Didn't you?"

Lewis shook his head. "I did it for me."

That hung in the air between them like fog refusing to lift.

"I needed to know," Lewis said, "that I could still do something right. That I could choose the harder thing."

Tom swallowed. "You did."

Neither spoke for a while. The sails strained against the wind in a slow, steady pull. The wounded schooner creaked beneath them like a living thing trying to remember how to move forward.

Finally, Tom stood. "We'll reach Delagoa in a week, they say. Maybe less, if the wind holds."

Lewis nodded.

As Tom turned to go, he paused. "If you ever find your boy... tell him he has your spine."

Lewis let out a slow breath. "If I find him, I won't need to tell him. I'll just show him."

Tom walked away. Not fast. But not skulking either.

Lewis looked out across the pale sea, the wind brushing his face like memory. He had lost much. But something had come back to him in the night—a sliver of dignity, not granted but earned. And that would carry him farther than any sail.

CHAPTER 23

They left the Mpondo settlement at first light, packs lightened but spirits heavier. The warning from the village elder still clung to John's ears like a fog. "The Zulu eat even the brave." William had translated it quietly, without embellishment, but the look in his eyes had said more.

The Mpondo had urged them to skirt north and east, following a gentler slope toward a river valley—but that would take them days off course. John had thanked them sincerely, shaking hands with those who offered them dried cassava and a pouch of maize meal, but he'd known even then that they would not heed the warning. The crew of the Mary was counting on him to assemble a hasty rescue and get medicines back to them. And beyond that, some unspoken drive had taken hold of him again—something older than maps or caution.

William didn't argue. He simply read the weather and the tracks, and then turned his body to face the land.

The trail they trudged turned to dry rock and rust-colored scrub, then vanished altogether. Midday brought a stretch of hardpan that blistered underfoot. William shifted to walking barefoot again. "Easier to feel the signs," he said. John followed suit until he gashed his heel on a hidden thorn and returned to boots.

By early evening, the wind came down off the high veldt with a restless chill. They moved into a shallow depression littered with old acacia stumps, and William gestured that they should make camp. The sky was cloudless, but something about the stillness set John on edge. No frogs. No birds. Just wind and bone-dry leaves.

They built the fire high and close, feeding it regularly with brittle twigs and roots dug up. They ate sparingly—roasted maize and a sliver of cured meat—and spoke little. John tried not to think about how many rounds were left in his powder satchel. He had counted them this morning. The barrel was now clean and dry again. But the number weighed on him like a dwindling heartbeat.

"You notice the silence?" he said, voice low.

William nodded. "Something stalks. Maybe just wind bringing stories. Maybe not."

John looked into the fire, the dancing shadows casting elongated forms across the rocks. They were still seated close when the first sound came—a low yowling snarl, then the unmistakable cackle of a hyena. One, then two, then more. The sound was near and unashamed.

John reached instinctively for his musket.

"Don't fire yet," William whispered, placing a hand on his arm. "They'll test. Fire only breaks silence once."

They stood slowly, circling the fire, their backs nearly touching. The brush trembled. Pale eyes flickered in the dark beyond the firelight. One beast emerged—a lanky shape, its coat mottled, head low and jaws slack. Its gait was awkward but quick. Then another, farther out.

John raised his musket as one of them let out a throaty whoop and edged closer, circling in a wide arc. William hissed and threw a flaming branch. The hyena recoiled but didn't run. Another laugh came from the right.

"They're too hungry," William said. "Even fire may not stop them tonight."

John's throat was dry. "Then we fight." In his mind, he knew that he had outfought an eagle, but then remembered there'd been only one.

The night stretched on, hour after hour, while the fire hissed and cracked like the breath of some tired beast. John dozed in brief snatches, never more than a few minutes at a time, his back against William's and the musket across his lap. Every rustle in the bush snapped his eyes open. Every breeze felt like movement.

William barely slept at all. He sat still and upright, gaze fixed beyond the firelight, jaw clenched as if holding some internal battle at bay. When John murmured something—he never remembered what—William only said, "Don't close your eyes. Not yet."

The hyenas didn't come back, but their presence remained. Their scent lingered like a curse on the wind. Now and then, a distant whoop echoed over the hills, low and taunting, as if mocking their wakefulness.

They fed the fire with every scrap of dry wood they had. He could feel the heat against his face, and still he shivered.

Around midnight, the wind shifted. Cooler air crept in from the east, and the sounds of the bush changed. The tension seemed to drain slightly, though neither of them said it aloud.

"They're gone," William murmured sometime near dawn. "But others will come."

John nodded, lips cracked, eyes raw. "We need to move early."

"We'll go when there's light."

And they waited, breathing smoke and fear until the first hint of gray bloomed along the horizon.

The next day tromped straight through into the brittle afternoon heat, which made the skin peel at the back of the neck and pulled sweat even from under the eyes. William paused now and then to adjust the musket slung across his shoulder. John tried to walk with the rifle reversed—barrel-down, to keep it from collecting more grit. Neither spoke much. The shadows of knobthorns were jagged and sparse, the grass brittle beneath their feet.

By dusk, they had made it to the rim of a low ravine, where scrub grew thicker and a spring trickled between flat stones. The place felt defensible, so they made camp—no fire, just cold meat and fingers of dried fig from a pouch. It was John who insisted they try sleeping in shifts. "I don't like the way the trees move when there's no wind," he said.

William nodded, uncharacteristically quiet.

It was John's shift when the rustling began. Not the hush of breeze or bird or leaf-drop, but something heavier. At first he thought it was wind shifting stones, but then came the growl.

Eyes blinked open in the dark.

A shape stepped out of the underbrush—then another. Low, sinewy. Shoulders hunched unnaturally forward. Yellow eyes glinted just beyond the circle of moonlight. Hyenas again.

John hissed for William, who rolled onto his knees and had the musket primed before fully awake. There were at least five that they could see, maybe more just out of view.

"They're bold," William whispered. "Devils."

John's fingers shook as he grasped for the powder horn. "Do we run?"

"Not with that leg," William said, nodding toward John's still-swollen ankle. "And not from hyenas. You run, they chase."

John nodded grimly. He tore a length of canvas and began twisting it into a torch as William used the last of their oil to soak a scrap of linen. When they lit it, the fire hissed and flared—but the hyenas only flinched.

"Still they come," William muttered. "Fire means nothing tonight."

One darted forward, teeth flashing. John fired—missed again. The shot rang out through the trees, the musket jumping in his hands. Smoke blurred his vision. The hyenas yelped and scattered—briefly—but then circled closer, bolder than before.

"Reload," William said urgently, pressing the powder horn into John's hands. "But make every shot count."

John's fingers flew. He had practiced for this—dry drills in the barn back home. Still, under pressure, the motions were clumsy.

Another hyena lunged. William swung the torch with a roar, landing a glancing blow to its side. The creature yelped and spun, retreating.

A moment later, John had the musket up again.

He aimed.

Fired.

This time the round struck true. One of the hyenas dropped mid-lunge, legs folding under it like sticks. The others backed off again—but not far.

"They'll return," William said grimly. "They've tasted fear, not defeat."

So they sat back-to-back, torch guttering between them, musket cradled and ready. Around them, the eyes continued to blink in the dark.

When a high-pitched bark echoed from the far end of the ravine, William cursed.

"What?" John asked.

"Jackals," William said. "Drawn to blood. They'll scavenge what's left of us if we die, but only after the hyenas are done."

John wiped sweat from his brow and tried not to think about what that meant.

The night dragged on like a fever dream—half-wakeful, half-blind with dread. The torch dwindled to an embered stub in William's hand, and even that light grew too faint to hold the hyenas back.

John loaded again by touch. His hands trembled as he poured powder into the pan and tamped the wad with trembling fingers. Each time, he told himself it was the last shot they'd need. Each time, the unnerving growls and grunts and clucks returned.

A pair of yellow eyes darted forward and back, gauging distance. Another shape flanked them silently. These awkward monsters were coordinated now—testing, learning. They were not just scavengers but strategists. The pack wanted blood.

"Shoot only when they lunge," William murmured.

John nodded, jaw clenched.

When the next charge came, it was sudden and low. The hyena bounded from the left, teeth bared, eyes wide with wild hunger.

John waited, counted the steps.

One. Two. *Fire*.

The creature flipped sideways in mid-leap, struck dead in its momentum. Its body skidded across the dirt with a dull, lifeless thud.

William surged to his feet and waved the dying torch over the corpse. "See what happens?" he shouted to the pack. "You want that?"

The hyenas hesitated.

Then came the jackals.

Three of them—smaller, leaner, bold. They slid into the outskirts of the standoff like side-thieves, pacing along the edge of the blood-scented dust. One yipped, a high barking call that made John's skin crawl. It wasn't just sound. It was laughter.

One of the hyenas turned and snapped at a jackal, driving it back. But another moved in from the far side, sniffing at the dead hyena. William raised a stone and hurled it with force. The jackal bolted, but not far.

"We're not going to sleep tonight, are we?" John asked through dry lips.

"No," William said flatly. "And we'll be lucky to see dawn."

John's musket was reloaded again. He'd lost count of the rounds left.

They sat pressed against each other, guarding each flank. All night the circle held—predators drifting forward and falling back, emboldened by exhaustion. Only the occasional stone toss kept them at bay.

Once, just before first light, a hyena charged again—desperate this time, reckless. John fired on instinct. The shot grazed its side, wounding but not killing. It fled shrieking.

And still they circled.

Dawn didn't break so much as seep in—slow and sullen, a pale wash of light bleeding across the scrub. The jackals were gone. The hyenas, too, vanished into the gray hush of early morning as if they'd never been there.

John stood stiffly, every joint protesting. His musket felt fused to his hands. How many rounds left? He rechecked the pouch. Just one more.

Beside him, William crouched over the torn hyena corpse, inspecting its mottled hide and broken teeth. "This one was old," he muttered. "Desperate. No wonder they came so close."

John rubbed his eyes. "Is this normal?"

"No," William said, rising. "Not this bold. Not for hyenas."

They packed up in silence. The fire had burned low during the night, and they left it to smolder in a ring of stones. John felt it in his legs—the heavy drag of fatigue, like wet sand clinging to his muscles. But there was no time for rest. The smell of blood was in the earth. Other creatures would come.

They walked without speaking for nearly an hour, keeping to the low rises where the ground was drier. Birdsong returned gradually. A flicker of sun pierced the clouds, and they both paused, then turned their faces to it like starving men glimpsing food.

"I don't think the Mpondo understand how bad things are out here," John said at last.

William made a quiet sound. "They understand. They just hoped you'd turn around."

John didn't reply. The river that had seemed so clear and abundant now felt impossibly far away. The land ahead—green in patches but dry in others—rolled out like a map no one had finished drawing.

"Next water?" John asked.

William tilted his head, considering. "Half-day's walk. If the stream hasn't dried up."

"If it has?"

"Then we ration what we've got."

John looked down at his water gourd. It felt light.

They moved on.

By midmorning, the ground changed again. The soil darkened, and thornbushes gave way to scattered trees. Animal tracks were more frequent—antelope and something larger, maybe a kudu. William knelt often, checking spoor. He walked as if the earth told him secrets.

John followed, musket slung across his shoulder, eyes scanning. Every rustle made his heart jump. His ears ached from listening so hard.

A sound—snapping brush—made them freeze.

But it was only a troop of tiny vervet monkeys, watching from the branches like smug sentries. One hurled a nut at John and chattered.

"Your cousins," William muttered with a rare smile.

John rolled his eyes. "Ugly lot, they are."

But the tension eased a little, and they walked on.

The stream, when they found it, was still flowing—just barely. More of a muddy trickle than a proper flow, but water nonetheless. They drank, filtered what they could, and filled the gourds. William found wild sorrel growing along the banks and they chewed the tart leaves, grateful for the taste.

As they sat, legs in the water, John asked, "How far now?"

William didn't answer right away. He looked east, then south. Then back at John. "Farther than I hoped," he said. "But we're closer now than we were yesterday. That counts for something."

John nodded slowly. "And tomorrow?"

William's face was void of expression. "We keep walking."

CHAPTER 24

The heat that afternoon pressed down like iron left in the sun—unrelenting, searing, and close. John's shirt was soaked through, his hair plastered to his forehead. Even William, who rarely complained, walked slower now, head down and shoulders slack beneath the rope-wrapped bundle of provisions.

They crested a low ridge of cracked ochre stone and paused.

Below them lay a shallow basin fed by a muddy trickle of stream. At its center, a stagnant pool gleamed in the sun, green at the edges but deep brown near the middle. Dragonflies danced above it in lazy figure eights. A warthog bolted at the sight of them, but nothing else stirred.

"A waterhole," John murmured, already loosening his pack. "Looks clean enough."

William said nothing at first. His eyes scanned the banks, then the stillness of the far shore.

"I wouldn't," he said finally. "Not yet. Could be hippos."

"Hippos?" John asked. "Here?"

William gave him a sideways glance. "They like places like this. Quiet. Hidden. Deep enough to sink in."

John peered into the water. It didn't seem large enough to hide something the size of a horse, let alone one of the great beasts William described. "I don't see anything."

"That's the trick," William said. "You never do."

But John was already slipping off his boots, rolling up his trouser legs. "Just to cool off," he muttered. "Not going in far."

William gave a tight frown but didn't stop him. Instead, he walked the perimeter slowly, stick in hand, watching the reeds for movement.

John waded in. The muddy bottom sucked gently at his feet, but the water felt blissful, even if it stank faintly of algae and dung. He splashed it over his chest, sighing aloud.

That's when the pool erupted.

A column of water shot into the air just ten paces to his right, followed by a guttural *roar*—a sound like a lion with its throat submerged. A massive gray bulk exploded from beneath the surface, its head broad as a barrel, mouth gaping open to reveal two tusk-like teeth longer than John's forearm.

"Get out!" William's voice cracked the air.

John screamed. The hippo surged forward, surprisingly fast for something so huge, churning water into foam.

John turned and scrambled toward shore, slipping once, then again as the bottom gave way. The hippo lunged, jaws snapping shut with a sickening *crack* just behind him.

Then William was there—howling, waving his arms, hurling a rock the size of a melon at the beast's flank.

It struck home. The hippo bellowed, veering sideways with a splash, and William grabbed John's arm, yanking him free of the shallows. They fell together on the muddy bank, panting, soaked, shaking. The hippo lingered for a moment at the water's edge, blowing spray from its nostrils, then sank beneath the surface with barely a ripple.

John coughed. His leg was scraped bloody where a rock had gouged him. His chest rose and fell like a bellows.

"That thing tried to kill me," he gasped.

William said nothing.

They sat side by side in silence, the stink of the waterhole curling around them.

"I thought they were… peaceful. You know. Like oxen."

William spat into the dirt. "Oxen don't open their mouths that wide. And they don't kill more men in Africa than lions."

John winced as he inspected his leg. The skin was torn, but the bleeding had slowed.

"I didn't think—"

"I know."

John looked up.

William's voice was quiet. "I've made mistakes too. Just don't make the same one twice."

They limped back up the ridge, leaving the waterhole behind.

They didn't stop moving until the sun was starting to set. Even then, John kept glancing behind them, half-expecting another ripple to break the surface of the water, another bellow to shake the reeds.

"I didn't know," he muttered, still breathless. "I didn't know they could move like that."

William nodded but said little. His shoulders were tense, his eyes scanning the terrain ahead as if expecting danger to come not from the water this time, but from the land.

They found a hollow near a cluster of dry, fan-leaved palms. Not ideal—too close to the water for comfort—but John's legs felt like driftwood, his shirt was soaked with sweat and fear. William gathered branches without a word, snapping kindling from a downed limb, his motions curt and practiced. He built a modest fire with care, feeding it slowly, letting it breathe.

John sat nearby, hugging his knees. "You should've let me drown," he said at last, voice cracking dry from the sun. "I'm just slowing us down. You'd be better off without me."

William tossed another stick into the flames. "Yes," he said flatly.

John winced, nodding. "Then why didn't you?"

William didn't speak right away. The fire crackled.

"I didn't," he said at last, "because you are not nothing to me."

John looked up. William didn't meet his eyes. He kept feeding the fire, deliberate and quiet.

Evening came soft and orange, shadows long and the air slightly cooler. They boiled what water they had, chewed the last of their dried meat, and laid their blankets out in the sand. John offered to take first watch.

William shook his head. "I'll do it. You sleep."

"You sure?"

"I slept this morning while we moved."

John frowned, unsure if it was a joke. But exhaustion got the better of him, and he crawled to the edge of the firelight and lay down. The last thing he saw was the dark blur of William's shape against the glow, sitting upright, alert.

He slept hard, deep, without dreams.

When he opened his eyes, the sun was already up. The fire had burned to cinders. But there was no sign of William.

John sat up fast. "William?" Silence.

He scrambled to his feet. The hollow was empty. No packs disturbed, no signs of struggle—but no footprints either, not fresh ones. Just vague traces of movement, already softening under the wind and heat.

John turned in a slow circle. "William!"

The trees rustled gently, indifferent.

A pit formed in his stomach. He moved out from the clearing, scanning the brush and trail beyond. Still nothing.

He turned back to the fire. William's small leather pouch, the one with his flint and beads, was gone. But John's pack had not been touched. And that scared John more than anything.

Panic coiled up in him. William wouldn't just leave. Not without a word. Not after all they'd endured. A dozen possibilities crowded his mind—kidnapping, animal attack, desertion, some errand gone wrong. But none of them came with answers. Only fear.

After an hour of waiting and whispering into the wind, he shouldered his pack, gripped his musket, and moved on alone.

He quickly discovered how much he'd relied on William.

The path they'd carved together now seemed to fold into uncertainty. Every step felt wrong. The sun was no comfort, burning overhead without hint of direction. His water was low. His mouth dry. Even the sound of his boots in the soil unnerved him—too loud, too final.

Birds flitted between branches with sudden cries that made him jump. A cluster of monkeys shadowed him from the trees, their black eyes curious and strange. One dropped from a low limb and scuttled across the trail, barking at him like a challenge. John swung the musket up but didn't fire. They were just animals.

He stopped only twice all day—to sip water and rub a blister that had opened on his shoulder where the musket strap rubbed. The land here rolled in waves of dry scrub and thornbush broken only by stretches of red soil and occasional rocky outcrops. The silence was not comforting. It felt watchful.

By late afternoon, his legs ached and the sweat on his back had dried into crusted salt. He climbed a slow rise to what he hoped might be a better vantage point, his musket slung across his other shoulder, boots dragging through brittle grass.

At the crest, he stopped dead.

Below him, the landscape changed completely.

It was a basin—broad, green at its heart, ringed by thorn trees and split by a winding brown river. Along one bank, nestled into the curve of the hills, stood a vast encampment. Hundreds of thatched domes—beehive huts—rose like clustered mushrooms. Fires crackled between them. Men moved with order and rhythm, tending to weapons, cooking, sharpening spears.

A ring of shields—large, oval, cowhide—lined a central clearing. The warriors near them stood tall and bare-chested, their heads bound in bands of fur, their limbs gleaming with oil. They practiced in formation, stamping feet in unison, ululating in sharp bursts that carried faintly on the wind.

It was the Zulu.

Even from this distance, John recognized the discipline, the raw power. He had heard of the Zulu army before—how it moved like one body, how it struck without mercy.

And then he saw the second camp.

Across the basin, on the opposite ridge, rose another cluster of huts—smaller but bristling with activity. The men there wore different ornaments—eagle feathers, heavier cloth wraps, and longer spears. Their banners were different too, darker with blue-black markings.

William had spoken their name once.

Ndwandwe.

A chill rippled down John's spine. These weren't just two large groups of warriors living side by side. They were poised. Watching each other. Waiting. And there were at least a thousand warriors on each side.

A war was coming.

And John Ross had wandered into the shadow of its storm.

CHAPTER 25

They had almost stopped watching the sea.

Nearly three weeks had passed since John and William had vanished up the coast, and though the *Mary* still clung to the sandbar like a carcass washed too far ashore, hope had mostly bled out of the men left behind.

The sun blistered everything it touched. The breeze blew steady from the east, but it carried no promise. Even the gulls had stopped circling—until the lookout gave a strangled cry. "Ship!"

A rustle of movement. Men scrambled to their feet, eyes squinting into the haze beyond the breakers.

There—just a pale smudge at first, then the clean outline of canvas. A schooner. Twin masts. Deep in the water. Cutting the current hard and fast, but far out—too far.

The carpenter let out a curse. "She's not comin' near. Takin' the deeper pass, she is. Must know about the shoals."

"Get smoke up!" someone shouted. "Flags—something!"

They shoved damp driftwood into the old firepit. Sparks hissed. Smoke trickled, then puffed—but the wind shifted inland, catching the signal and dragging it uselessly toward the dunes.

Then—"Wait," murmured one of the younger lads, eyes locked on the schooner's deck. "That sail. That red trim on the foresail. I saw it before. Back in the Cape."

He glanced at Galloway, the first mate. "That's *her*, sir. That's the *Maria Louisa*."

Galloway froze. "You're certain?"

"She sometimes docks near us. I know her name. I swear it."

A silence. A long, bitter silence.

Galloway looked down the beach, where the last of the casks had been buried against rot. He looked toward the dunes, where the sick lay under flies and fevered dreams.

The *Maria Louisa*—and Lewis Ross—passed them by, no more than a shadow on the sea.

Someone fired a shot into the air, a desperate crack. Another flung his arms wide, waving a strip of white sailcloth from the top of a stripped pole. But the schooner did not slow. Did not turn.

Did not see them.

By the time the sun tipped westward, the ship had vanished behind the horizon.

They would never know how close they had come.

Two days later, the schooner *Maria Louisa* dropped anchor just after dawn, its sails slack and salt-stiffened, its hull grimed with the long pull northward. Lewis Ross stood near the rail with the aid of his crutch, blinking into the haze that blurred sea and land alike. This was Delagoa Bay, the place that had haunted John's stories and Lewis's dreams—his final hope, perhaps. But it was no city of gold.

The shoreline was low and marshy, stitched with mangroves that reached crooked fingers toward the tide. Beyond them, a few scattered buildings—some wooden, some stone—clung to the soil like they feared it might slip from beneath them. There was no town square, no crowd to greet them. Just a cluster of dwellings half-choked by mist and silence. This place was unlike the fantasy town

Lewis had described to John and was barely changed since that long-ago time when Lewis had set foot here.

"Not much to look at," said the captain beside him, chewing a wedge of dried meat. "But it's what's here. Portuguese mostly, a few Dutch traders. Some don't last long."

Lewis nodded faintly. "Zulu country not far inland, is it?"

The captain spat over the rail. "Too damn close. You hear drums sometimes at night. Loud ones. Or see the smoke from burned homesteads. They never say it's Zulu, not out loud—but everyone knows."

Lewis swallowed and said nothing more. His stomach churned, though whether from seasickness or dread he couldn't say.

They came ashore by small boat, landing on a muddy slip near a warped wooden jetty. A Portuguese trader with a pitted musket slung over his back eyed them suspiciously, then waved them toward a customs shed fashioned from driftwood and brick. Paperwork was filled out slowly. No one smiled.

"Any news of a red-haired boy?" Lewis asked quietly of a younger clerk who looked less scowling than the rest.

The clerk blinked at him. "A red-haired boy?"

"He would've come by land. Young. Scottish. About thirteen by now."

The man shook his head. "No one like that. Not here."

Lewis stood in the sticky heat and let the words settle. *No one like that.* He had no real reason to believe John had made it this far, but still the hope had stuck itself in him like a tick. Now it was gone, and he didn't know what to do with the hollow it left.

He spent the rest of the day wandering the outer edges of the settlement. It wasn't much. A few houses built high on stilts to survive flooding. One stone church with a cracked bell. Traders with wary eyes and rifles always within reach. He caught whispers in broken Dutch and Portuguese. One name came up again and again, usually low and urgent—*Shaka*. The great king. The lion of the Zulu.

No one dared speak of Shaka in detail, but the silence that followed the name told Lewis all he needed. *They lived in fear.* Even here, on this swampy fringe of empire, the shadow of Shaka was felt. No one knew when his warriors might come, and the uncertainty made every drumbeat from the interior feel like thunder.

By dusk, Lewis had nothing but his coat, his crutch, and the dull ache of exhaustion. He found a cheap cot in a rundown lodging house near the bay, the kind of place where no questions were asked. The room stank of mildew and sweat. He didn't care.

That night, as crickets whirred and drums echoed faintly across the water, Lewis Ross lay awake and tried to picture his son's face— but found it already fading.

Lewis rose before dawn the next morning. He shaved with a rusty blade over a basin of rainwater and put on his patched coat—one sleeve pinned, one pantleg rolled and bound for balance. He looked like a castoff soldier from some forgotten war, but he stood straighter than he had in years.

No work had been offered, but he went down to the docks anyway. Laborers were already hoisting crates of dried fish and salted hides onto ox-carts bound for Mozambique interior posts. A Portuguese trader with gray whiskers and a broad straw hat watched the scene with a practiced eye.

"You need a man?" Lewis asked.

The trader squinted. "You have only one arm and one leg."

"I can count. Take inventory. And I don't cheat."

The man studied him, shrugged. "You pay your own food?"

Lewis nodded.

The man tossed him a battered ledger. "Start with the dried cod. Don't lose the chalk."

That was the beginning. For the next three days, Lewis worked the warehouse and dock manifest under the names of men whose faces he barely saw. He recorded sacks of grain, weighed bundles of cloth, and scrawled entries in a mix of English and poor Portuguese. It was hot, dull work, but it kept him from thinking too long in one direction. At night he returned to the same rented cot and listened to the hoots and cries of unknown creatures. Still no word of John. Not from any incoming trader, not from the mission outposts that trickled in with weather-beaten messengers.

The town had no real core. It was more like a wound—slow to heal, never fully scabbed over. Each day brought new rumors. That the Zulu had raided a Portuguese station upriver. That an English trader had vanished two weeks inland. That a missionary caravan had been spared only because they carried a French flag. Most of these stories ended the same way—fire, loss, silence.

By the fifth day, Lewis sat at a makeshift canteen with a wooden mug of watery tea and a heel of bread. Across from him sat an older man—bald, rail-thin, and with a grimace that passed for a smile.

"You're not from here," the man said.

Lewis shook his head. "Scotland."

"Looking for someone?"

"My son. Red hair. Thirteen. May have come up the coast from the Cape."

The man grunted. "Haven't seen him. But if he went north.... if he passed near Zulu lands... well, I'd stop looking."

Lewis's grip on his cup tightened. "You sayin' he's dead?"

"I'm saying the Zulu don't forget strangers. Especially white ones." He leaned forward. "You're lucky you got here at all."

"Then why do you stay?"

The man barked a joyless laugh. "Because there's nowhere else to go."

That night, Lewis dreamed of mist and fire. Of a boy running barefoot along a jungle trail, outpacing the drums but not the shadow that followed. He woke with sweat in his eyes and the knowledge that no one had yet seen John.

Still, he stayed.

The rain began in the middle of the week—long, slanted sheets that blurred the line between ocean and sky. It soaked the red earth roads, turned gullies to streams, and hung like a gray curtain over Delagoa Bay. Lewis worked anyway. The docks didn't stop for rain.

He had begun to walk the perimeter of the settlement at dusk. Not out of duty, but because he couldn't sit still. The waiting had turned to ache. He studied every face that passed through the port. At the arrival of each schooner or ox-cart convoy, he stood near the disembarking men like a cast-iron figure, hoping to see a familiar shock of red hair—or even to hear his name.

Nothing.

One evening, as the rain broke for an hour of pale light, Lewis walked out toward the edge of the settlement. The jungle loomed just two hundred yards beyond the last cluster of huts and fencing— dense, unknowable, whispering with insects and the wind. A few men with rifles passed him on the trail, their faces hard.

"You looking to go inland?" one of them called.

Lewis hesitated. "Maybe."

The man stopped and looked him over. "You won't last a week. Not with that leg. You got people out there?"

"My son."

The man nodded slowly, then gave a grim smile. "Then you've already lost more than most."

They moved on. Lewis remained.

The jungle tempted him like an impending answer. As if its wildness could somehow yield up his boy. He imagined pushing into the green, musket in one hand, heart beating like a war drum, demanding the bush surrender his son. But it was a fantasy—and not just because of his missing limbs. Even whole men didn't return from that inland unknown. Portuguese outposts vanished without a trace. English explorers went silent after a single season. And the Zulu were not a myth. Everyone here spoke of them with fear rooted in truth.

That night, as thunder rolled far off, Lewis lay in his cot with his eyes wide. The room was dark but alive with his thoughts. He imagined John alive—sunburned and limping, maybe—but clever, strong, moving carefully southward.

If I go, he thought, and John comes here, he'll find nothing. He'll think I gave up.

The decision formed not in words, but in the slow calming of his limbs. He would not go inland. He would not chase a shadow. He would wait.

If his son was alive, he would find this place. If not—

Lewis turned on his side and faced the wall, jaw tight.

He would wait anyway.

CHAPTER 26

John crouched in a cluster of low scrub near the lip of a rise, not daring to move, barely breathing. His heart was already pounding, but it had nothing to do with fear of being found. What he saw before him stole the words from his mind and froze them behind his eyes.

Two armies.

Two great, living seas of warriors, stretching from one horizon to the other, facing one another across a shallow expanse of yellow earth and scattered thornbush. Smoke drifted slowly from cooking fires. Shields gleamed darkly in the haze. From one side, the Zulu regiments stood in rows as rigid and symmetrical as wheat furrows, divided by color and age, each unit identifiable by distinct headdress and shield pattern. On the opposite end, the Ndwandwe forces— more loosely formed, more colorful, and yet no less fierce-looking— gathered in a massive half-circle, their warriors adorned with beads, feathers, and body paint.

No one moved.

John pressed his chest into the cool earth and stared, eyes wide.

He had never imagined so many people gathered without houses or wagons or churches or livestock. No banners flew. No horses stomped. These were not armies like those of Europe. They were more ancient than that. Primal. Elemental. And yet, there was nothing chaotic about what the Zulus were doing.

From their end of the field came a low, rhythmic chant.

"Bayete," a voice murmured to John's left, barely within earshot.

John startled and turned—but it was only an old man, seated far below in the grasses, painted with white ash and gazing at the field with the detachment of a prophet. John hadn't noticed him before.

"Bayete," the man repeated, as if the word explained everything. The word lodged in his memory.

The Zulu regiments were beginning to move. But not forward. They moved *within themselves*—shifting formation, tightening the horned crescent shape that William had once described. The chest in the middle. The horns on the sides. The loins hidden behind.

It was a war design.

Across the field, the Ndwandwe answered the chant with a bellow of their own—raw, wilder. A beating of shields. A rising hum. Then whistles. Then howls.

The Zulus stood unmoving, a black wall of resolve.

John's mouth had gone dry. He swallowed.

Now came the paint.

In the basin's center, Ndwandwe warriors began stripping bare to the waist and painting their skin in stripes of red and ochre. One man smeared white clay across his face like a skull and danced in circles, spinning his spear above his head. Another drove his blade into the earth and screamed into the sky, chest heaving, legs quaking in a war-dance that seemed more convulsion than ritual.

And then drums. Deep ones. Not Western. No brass or snare. Just heavy, skin-stretched drums thumped by open hands or sticks the size of arms.

Boom. Boom. *Boom.*

The sound vibrated in John's ribs. Each note a summons.

He felt a flush of terror rise to his throat. This wasn't spectacle. This wasn't theater. These men were not pretending to go to war.

They were going to kill each other right here with weapons that didn't miss and shields that couldn't stop everything. And he would be here—watching—without the power to stop it, without the understanding to make sense of it.

He reached for the gourd at his side and took a single sip of water. His fingers trembled.

Below him, both sides had begun to move again, slower now, with increasing unity. A ripple of clicking sounds, like castanets or tongue clacks, passed through the Zulu ranks, and warriors struck their spears on their shields in a coordinated wave.

Click-click—thud. Click-click—thud.

Silence again.

And then a voice. Not a loud one, but high-pitched and sharp. A single Zulu commander's call. The ranks began to march. Slow, deliberate, synchronized.

John didn't know it yet, but he was watching the beginning of a true regimental formation in action—the very tactic that had made Shaka's empire nearly unstoppable. These were not warriors rushing into chaos. They were a blade being drawn.

The Ndwandwe saw it too. From their front line came a wild, piercing ululation, and then a dozen runners broke from the flanks to charge across the basin alone, erratic, testing.

The trap had been baited.

But John didn't know that either. He only knew that the world was about to shatter.

And he could not look away.

The runners didn't return. Whether they were cut down or fled behind the haze, John couldn't tell. The open field seemed to shimmer under the gathering heat, and the dust was already starting to lift. But something had changed. The ground had taken on a kind of charge— as if it was holding its breath beneath the weight of what was coming.

And then the *ululating* began.

From the far end of the basin—Ndwandwe side—rows of warriors began to *screech* in unison, their voices rising and falling like warbirds diving. Spears rattled against shields. Anklets made of bone and horn rang out as warriors stamped their feet. It was not music. It was a madness composed.

Then came the answering sound from the Zulu side.

Not screeching. Not high and wild. But deep and guttural. *Huh!... Huh!... Huh!* With every exhale, the Zulu warriors advanced a step. Their shields moved as one. Their chest formation advanced in time to the war-chant, a terrifying, pulsing mass that consumed the field like black oil.

John crouched lower, heart racing.

The horns of the Zulu army began to sweep outward—he had seen them curling away from the center an hour before, and now he understood why. The Zulu impis were not just moving in lines—they were shaping the field itself. Trapping the Ndwandwe in a crescent. Encircling them.

But the Ndwandwe weren't passive.

Just as the Zulu horns started to swing, the central mass of the Ndwandwe army surged forward with a scream. Hundreds of warriors broke into a run. No signal John could see had been given—only the scream, and they were off, bare feet pounding the earth in a frenzy of power and color. Spears aloft, faces painted, eyes wild.

They hit the Zulu chest like a wave smashing a cliff.

There was no great explosion of metal. No gunpowder. No smoke. Just the crunch of impact, the guttural cries of bodies slamming into shields, the sharp clatter of spears against cowhide. The sounds were organic, and yet somehow louder than any cannon.

John could not breathe.

From his perch, he saw the Zulu front line *bend*—but not break. The chest absorbed the blow, shield against shield, spears stabbing low in upward thrusts. The clash was brutal. Dozens fell immediately, trampled or struck. The earth turned red.

And now the horns came in.

The Zulu wings curled around the flanks of the Ndwandwe with terrifying speed, sweeping in like scythe blades. These warriors hadn't even *joined* the first clash yet—*they had been waiting*. And now they came with speed and purpose, flanking the disorganized rear of the Ndwandwe force. Trapped.

The screams shifted pitch. Panic crept into the Ndwandwe ranks. What had begun as a glorious charge now turned into a compression, their center caught and their flanks collapsing under pressure. Spears were thrown in desperation. Shields abandoned. But the Zulus came on.

John felt his jaw clench so tightly it ached.

There was no retreat. Not in this war.

He watched one Ndwandwe warrior break free and sprint toward a low rise, only to be intercepted by a Zulu fighter who flung his short spear—the iklwa, as William had named it in his stories. It was flung with such force it impaled the man through the belly. The scream that followed rang across the basin like a warning bell.

The field was a frenzy.

The Zulu discipline held. John could see commanders shouting commands—not by trumpet or flag, but with *gestures*, shouts, and formations learned by heart. The discipline was astonishing. Even as men fell, new fighters from the rear ranks surged forward to fill the gaps. Every movement fed the next.

John's hands were sweating. He clutched his musket, though it was useless. He was far from either force, a ghost in the grass, and yet the fear was real, the violence visceral.

Men bled. Men howled. The very *sky* seemed to recoil from the madness.

He had never seen this kind of war. No one in Scotland had ever described this. This wasn't redcoats and rebels. This was something older—older than history. Something born from land and blood and bone.

And somehow… he couldn't look away.

The Ndwandwe were being driven back now. He saw it. Their lines faltered, their warriors slipping in blood and dust. Shields dropped. Men fled. But there was nowhere to flee. The Zulu horn had closed. Escape was not part of the Zulu formation.

This battle was ending.

But John's terror was only beginning.

A cluster of Zulu warriors on the far side of the basin had broken from formation—intent not on the battlefield but on a single figure moving along the outer slope.

John.

He hadn't realized he'd shifted. He hadn't noticed that he'd risen to one knee, watching, exposed.

But *they* had seen.

And now they were coming for him—half a dozen, spears in hand, blood on their arms, eyes burning.

John Ross ran. His lungs burned. He crashed through tall grass, stumbling over roots, vaulting stones, his musket clutched tight in one hand as if it could still save him.

The shouts behind him grew louder, closing in. Zulu warriors—six, maybe more—were giving chase, and they weren't guessing. They were *tracking* him. Fast. Silent. Relentless.

He dodged into a narrow gully, hoping the brush might slow them down, but it only seemed to close the gap. He dared one glance over his shoulder—bad idea. A root caught his foot and he pitched forward, the air leaving his chest in a single, agonizing grunt His musket flew from his hand.

Before he could scramble to his knees, a heavy figure crashed into him from behind, driving his face into the dirt. Arms pinned. A second weight landed on his legs. He thrashed once, twice—but the pursuers were too strong. Trained.

Rough hands bound his wrists with leather thongs. One cf them rolled him over. A dark face loomed above, young but fierce, eyes rimmed in red paint, teeth bared in a sneer.

"He is red, his hair," the warrior said in a strange dialect, his voice low but amused. Another replied with something like a chuckle.

John struggled to understand. Zulu? No—something adjacent. Then he heard a more familiar voice.

"Don't kill him."

The order came first in Zulu, then in clean English, precise and calm, apparently for John's benefit.

The warriors froze. One backed off slightly as a tall figure emerged from the trees. He wore no weapons but carried himself with total command. His skin was deep umber, his bearing regal, and around his shoulders was a cloak woven of jackal tails and beadwork.

Speaking again in Zulu, this man continued. "I said, *do not kill him*. He is one of the whites Shaka must meet."

John blinked up at him, chest heaving. "Who... are you?"

The man smiled faintly. "Interpreter. For the King."

John's heart was a hammer now. "Shaka?"

The interpreter nodded. "He has asked to see all who walk in his lands and do not belong. He will especially want to see you with red hair, I would think."

The warriors yanked John to his feet.

The youngest one retrieved John's musket, holding it with visible confusion—he clearly didn't know what it was, only that it must matter.

They marched him back across the slope, away from the field of bodies, the sky now orange with dust and dying light. The Zulu dead were already being gathered. The Ndwandwe bodies lay sprawled, stripped of weapons, blood soaking the earth. Hyenas and jackals and scavenging birds were already enjoying dinner.

As they walked, John dared ask, "There was another... boy. With me."

The interpreter glanced at him, his gaze unreadable. "You may see him. Or you may not. The King decides."

John looked down at his feet—bruised, blistered, caked in dust. But he had been strong. He had not broken. He had run, but not begged. Not wept. He'd watched the battle. Stood on the edge of something vast and terrible and sacred. And he had not turned away.

Perhaps that was why they hadn't killed him.

Perhaps that was why the King would be interested in him.

They walked for hours, into hills crowned with thorn trees and thick shadows. Just as night threatened to swallow them whole, the fires appeared—torches, dozens of them, circling a great kraal like stars drawn to earth.

The King awaited.

And John Ross was being led into the lion's den.

CHAPTER 27

John had never seen anything like it.

The kraal—*KwaBulawayo*, as one of the guards murmured—rose in circular majesty from the crest of a shallow hill, an immense enclosure of sharpened stakes and high woven fencing. Hundreds of huts dotted its interior, arranged in concentric rings like ripples in a pond, their thatched roofs glistening with dew and firelight. Warriors moved in disciplined patterns through the gates and alleys, all armed, all silent.

John's entrance was not met with curiosity or derision. It was met with indifference. He was nothing here. Just a thin, red-haired boy in torn clothes dragged between towering men who could kill him with a glance.

But someone had said Shaka would want to see him.

That thought flickered in his mind like a candle in wind.

He was brought first to a low structure near the outer ring. It was more fortified than the rest, with a reed door and two older warriors standing guard. Inside, the air smelled of smoked hide and dry earth. They sat him down, offered no food, and left him. For hours, maybe longer. He drifted in and out of sleep.

When the door finally opened again, it was not the interpreter, but a woman.

She was older than he'd expected, her back straight, her movements smooth. She wore layered beadwork that glittered against her copper skin and looked at John as one might study a rare bird.

"You do not kneel?" she asked in a Zulu-accented English.

John blinked. "I wasn't told to."

She studied him a moment longer. "Interesting."

She brought a basin and placed it before him. Water—not warm, but clean. "You must wash. The King will see you at moonrise."

John hesitated. "Why?"

She looked amused. "Because he says so. That is enough, is it not?"

When she left, John washed quickly, grateful for the cold splash of water on his skin. He had no change of clothes, no way to hide the bruises and cuts, but he scrubbed as best he could. Something told him appearance mattered here. It wasn't about impressing anyone. It was about showing respect. Showing resilience.

At moonrise, they came for him.

This time the procession was formal—two spear-bearing warriors before him, two behind, and the interpreter once again at his side.

The kraal had come alive with the arrival of dusk. Drums beat in slow rhythm from somewhere beyond the main enclosure, and fire pits crackled with fresh flames. Dozens of warriors lined the path, eyes forward, faces unreadable. Not one looked at him.

John's throat was dry.

The interpreter said, "You will bow. Not grovel. Not fall on your face. Just bow."

"To show I'm not afraid?"

"To show you understand."

They reached the heart of the kraal—a great open circle of packed earth surrounded by fire poles and lined with seated warriors. A single figure stood at the far end, bare-chested, barefoot, taller than all the rest.

Shaka.

The name alone carried a weight John could feel in his chest.

The Zulu King wore a leopard-skin mantle and an elaborate headdress of feathers and beads. His eyes were narrow, fixed. His chest was broad and his arms corded with muscle. But what stunned John most was his stillness. Shaka didn't shift, didn't twitch He *waited*, motionless, like a predator before the spring.

John stepped forward as guided, reached the place where he had been instructed to stop—and bowed.

Low. Steady.

The drums stopped.

A beat of silence. Then Shaka spoke.

The voice was deep and smooth, like stone on stone. Measured. Commanding.

The interpreter echoed, "He says... you are not what he expected."

John straightened slightly, heart hammering. "I don't know what he expected."

A pause. Shaka smiled faintly. A warrior beside him laughed.

"He says—he expected fear. You walked into his kraal with the eyes of someone who knows death but does not run from it."

John blinked. "I've seen things. I've lost friends. But I don't want to die."

"He says—that is wise. But not the same as fear."

Shaka stepped down from his elevated place. The crowd hushed. Warriors leaned in.

The King approached.

He stood before John now, close enough that the boy could see the scars on his chest, the lines of paint across his arms, the gleam in his dark, calculating eyes.

Then he looked down—at John's feet. Bare. Callused. Cracked from weeks of travel. A strange flicker passed across Shaka's face.

"He says you walk like his men walk," the interpreter murmured. "With pain. And purpose."

Shaka raised one hand. A warrior stepped forward and offered a wooden spear—not to be thrown, but held ceremonially.

He extended it toward John.

The entire kraal seemed to hold its breath.

John hesitated, then slowly reached for it. He wrapped his fingers around the shaft.

The crowd exhaled, a chorus of murmurs and grunts of approval.

Shaka turned and walked away.

The interpreter leaned close. "The King says you will stay. You will not be harmed. He will decide what you are."

And just like that, the boy from Scotland was no longer a stranger. He was something else.

Something watched.

Something chosen.

John wasn't returned to the same reed hut. After his audience with Shaka, he was led deeper into the kraal, past rows of low huts and guarded enclosures, to a more secluded area beneath the shadow of a thorn-branched tree. A pair of warriors gestured silently toward a structure half-sunken into the slope of the earth—mud-walled, its doorway covered in woven matting.

He hesitated, then stepped inside.

At first, he saw only shadows and the vague glow of embers. Then a voice—gravelly, British—startled him.

"Well I'll be damned. You're just a boy."

John froze.

From the dark, a man stood up. Mid-thirties, wiry, with a reddish beard streaked gray and a bandaged arm. His shirt was once white. "You're not one of them."

"No," John said cautiously.

Another figure stirred near the back. "It's John," came a whisper. This voice was smoother, recognizable.

John turned, heart jolting. "William?"

The figure stepped into the light—thinner now, limping slightly, but it was him. William.

"I thought you were dead," John said hoarsely.

"I thought *you* were," William replied. "They took me when you were still sleeping. Left you there like you were invisible."

A third man, older and gaunt, rose slowly from the straw bedding. He looked at John with blank eyes, then offered a weak smile. "Captain Farewell," he said. "And this here's Doctor Fynn." He nodded toward the man with the bandaged arm.

John looked from face to face, stunned. "I thought you were killed—or worse."

"Oh, it's been worse," Fynn said. "But we're alive, for now."

The room was quiet for a moment.

"How long have you been here?" John asked.

"No idea, really," Farewell answered. "We were taken near the coast—no warning, no fight. Just… captured. The King wanted to question us."

"About what?"

Fynn exchanged a glance with Farewell. "Why we came. What we wanted. Whether we were spies for the Dutch or British Crown. Shaka doesn't trust easily—and he hates being lied to."

"But you told him the truth?"

"We told him what he wanted to hear," Fynn said grimly.

William shifted on his feet. "They treat us well enough. No torture. But the King plays his own long game. He's weighing us, measuring."

John sat down beside them, his muscles sore, his thoughts racing.

"They took me to him," he said. "Tonight. He looked at my feet, gave me a spear. Said I walk like his men."

Fynn raised his eyebrows. "He gave you a spear?"

"As a test, I think."

Farewell nodded slowly. "He's done that before. It's a mark. A way of saying, 'You're interesting. You're not dead yet.'"

A silence fell over the little cell. Outside, drums beat faintly in the distance.

John leaned forward. "Do you think we'll get out of here?"

Farewell didn't answer.

Fynn scratched at his bandage. "We might. If we're useful. If he decides we can be trusted. But the rules shift like sand here. One day you're a guest. The next..."

William cleared his throat. "Then we stay useful."

The others looked at him.

"We watch, we listen, we learn," William said. "And if the chance comes—we run."

John nodded. "Or we fight."

Fynn chuckled, a short, mirthless sound. "Spoken like someone who doesn't know how many warriors this man commands."

"I saw them," John said. "Thousands. I watched a battle. I saw what they did."

Farewell leaned forward, eyes intense. "Then you understand. You're no longer a passenger on some wrecked ship. You're in the eye of the storm now."

John met his gaze. "Then I'll stay standing."

Outside, a wind rose across the dry hills. In the distance, a horn blew—low and mournful.

Something was coming.

And for now, all they could do was wait.

CHAPTER 28

John woke with a start.

The reed hut was heavy with the damp breath of morning. For a moment, he didn't know where he was. Then, memory swept in like a tide—Shaka's warriors, the battle, the long walk under guard, and now this—a sleeping mat of woven rushes and a single open window through which the lowing of cattle echoed.

He sat up slowly, muscles stiff, unsure if he was allowed to move freely. But the entrance was open, and no one stood guard. The woven doorway rustled as someone approached. A young warrior appeared, silently gesturing for John to follow.

Outside, the light was soft and golden. The kraal was alive with movement—women tending fires, boys herding goats, warriors sharpening spears or oiling shields. The scale of it all stunned him. He'd seen villages, yes—but this was something else. This was a kingdom in miniature: a living engine of strength and ritual.

He was led through the compound to a wide, packed-earth clearing shaded by acacia trees. At its center stood Shaka.

The king was tall—taller than John remembered from their first meeting—and lean as a whip. His shoulders were draped in jackal-hide, his chest bare but painted with red ochre in sharp, angular patterns. Around him stood several izinduna—senior advisors—and, just behind, a man John had seen before. The interpreter.

Shaka raised a hand. John stopped several paces away.

The king's voice came, low and sonorous, in Zulu. The interpreter translated without delay.

"You were seen watching the battle."

"I didn't mean to," John said, then corrected himself. "I was looking for help. My friend—William—was taken."

The interpreter passed this on and received a response.

"He says you walked far," the interpreter told John. "Longer than any boy your size should have survived."

John didn't know what to say. He lowered his gaze.

Another murmur from Shaka.

The interpreter added: "He says your feet are like a warrior's. Hardened. You are not like the other whites."

That startled John. "I came here for my mother, who is very sick. To earn money so she could get better. But I—" He caught himself. "I never thought it would lead here."

Shaka turned his gaze toward the eastern hills, then back to John. A longer sentence followed. The interpreter hesitated before rendering it.

"He says mothers must be honored. A son who walks the wilderness for his mother... may be worth more than a thousand who stay in comfort."

The silence that followed was heavy but not cold.

Shaka gestured to one of the attendants, who brought forward a gourd of water and a rough cake of sorghum. John accepted them with both hands, bowed his head slightly, and drank.

Then the king spoke again.

"You will remain in the kraal," said the interpreter. "You are not a prisoner. But you are not free."

John nodded, grateful and unsettled all at once.

As he was led away, he felt Shaka's eyes still on him.

The days passed slowly but not unpleasantly. Within the high palisades of Shaka's kraal, John began to lose the sharp edge of fear. Though always under the eyes of guards, he was permitted to walk sections of the compound, to sit beneath a fig tree, or speak with the other captives—William, Farewell, and Fynn—during the midday meal or just before sunset. That much freedom felt like a blessing.

The four of them were not kept in chains, nor confined to a single hut, though warriors watched them from a distance. They were not free, but they were not mistreated.

John came to look forward to his brief conversations with William. The older boy was thinner, still wary, but his sharp wit hadn't dulled. "You've become a favorite of the king," William joked one afternoon. "Next you'll be wearing leopard skins and issuing commands."

Farewell, by contrast, remained withdrawn. He rarely spoke of anything beyond survival—how to avoid offending the Zulu, how to keep one's tone respectful but not weak. Fynn seemed to navigate the space between the two men, occasionally smiling at John and asking questions about how he'd ended up so far inland.

"You must be some kind of ghost," Fynn had said, shaking his head. "Not even the Zulu would expect a red-haired boy to crawl out of the forest."

On the fifth day of John's relative freedom, he was summoned again to Shaka's shade beneath the fig tree. The king sat on a carved wooden stool with two women beside him and a warrior whisking flies away with a cow-tail switch.

John approached with slow steps, his stomach tight. He bowed as he had seen others do and sat cross-legged where the interpreter pointed.

Shaka stared at him and then, through the interpreter, he spoke. "You have not run."

John met the king's gaze, then looked at the interpreter. "No, I have not. And I won't."

"You speak often with the others," came the next line.

"They are my friends," John said. "We came here by accident. We mean no harm."

There was a pause. Shaka gave a soft grunt and gestured to one of the women, who handed John a roasted yam and water.

John accepted both, heart pounding. For a time, Shaka did not speak. He turned to one of his commanders and gave a quiet order, and the warrior departed. The interpreter remained still, but watchful.

Finally, John gathered his courage and said, "May I ask something, great king?"

The question was passed along. Shaka did not respond immediately. He simply looked at John again with that curious intensity that made the boy feel transparent.

Then the reply: "Ask."

John took a breath. "If I have your trust enough to walk freely… might my friends be allowed the same? At least here, within the kraal. They are not soldiers. Only travelers."

The interpreter relayed the request.

Shaka's expression did not change, but his fingers moved slightly—perhaps a signal, perhaps a thought. Then he said something curt in Zulu.

The interpreter turned. "They will not leave the kraal. But yes. They may walk as you do. Speak as you do. Under watch."

Relief surged in John's chest.

"Thank you," he said.

Shaka tilted his head, then spoke again—low, almost amused. The interpreter translated: "You speak with fire. Like a warrior. But you are not one."

"No," John admitted. "But I've walked far. I didn't come for war. I came to earn coin—for my mother. She's sick, as you know—dying, I think—far away. I had no other way."

Shaka said nothing for a moment. Then, quietly, he replied in his own tongue, and the interpreter spoke: "Then, perhaps your journey has meaning."

And with that, the king rose and walked away, his shadow long across the dry earth.

John remained seated beneath the fig tree, the half-eaten yam warm in his hand, wondering if the wind had just shifted in his favor.

The days stretched into weeks.

  John marked time by the changes in the light, by the slant of the shadows on the palisade, and by the routines of life inside the kraal. Morning chants gave way to midday drills, and the long hush of evening settled over the huts like a ritual. He had learned not only the rhythms but also the rules—when to speak, when to bow, when to be invisible. But he was no longer treated as a prisoner. He was—something else. Watched. Measured. Endured, and occasionally, included.

Shaka had not yet spoken again through the interpreter since the day John requested that William, Fynn and Farewell be allowed to roam freely. But the king had nodded—slowly—and that was enough. The three had been given certain liberties, though none dared stray far. They shared a hut now, one of the smaller reed structures on the outer ring of the kraal. John visited often.

Farewell was already fading—his cough had deepened, and he walked with a tilt, one shoulder higher than the other, as if permanently braced against a wind no one else could feel. Fynn, ever the doctor, was trying what he could with local herbs, but even he seemed resigned. William, thinner now and quieter, had taken on the role of their steady guardian, often emerging from the hut to meet John with a tired but loyal smile.

"You're not just surviving," William said once, sitting beside John as the sun set behind the kraal. "You're being studied. Like a bird that sings in the wrong forest."

"Maybe," John murmured. "But if the bird sings long enough, maybe the forest learns the tune."

It was around that time that the Zulu boy appeared.

He was tall for his age—perhaps twelve or thirteen—and moved like a shadow slipping through firelight. The other boys in the kraal gave him wide berth. His name, whispered from one mouth to another, was Langa. John learned later that it meant "sun," though it seemed an ironic name for one who carried himself like dusk. His father, the whispers went, had been a great warrior who died with distinction, and Shaka had taken the boy into his inner circle as a kind of foster son.

For many days, Langa said nothing. He simply appeared—watching John from a distance, sometimes mimicking his actions, sometimes tossing pebbles in quiet patterns at the edge of the hut. One afternoon, when John was helping prepare a simple stew near the fire, Langa dropped beside him and wordlessly began chopping roots.

"Don't say anything," William whispered later that night. "He chose you. No one chooses him."

At first, their friendship was built on gestures. John would show him how to tie a Scottish-style knot. Langa would demonstrate a silent hunting signal. They shared bits of food, traded carved trinkets, and finally, one evening, shared a laugh—an awkward, high-pitched thing that startled both of them.

It was that laugh that drew Shaka's attention.

He had been seated in the central circle, surrounded by warriors, watching sparring practice. When he heard the sound, he turned, eyes narrowing as he saw Langa nudging John with a carved stick shaped like a miniature spear.

He said something low to his interpreter, who returned a moment later with the words, "You have stirred the lion's cub."

John stiffened. "Have I offended him?"

The interpreter shook his head slowly. "No. The cub does not play unless he feels safe. The lion watches."

From that day forward, Shaka would occasionally observe them—never speaking, never interrupting, but always nearby. The other boys began to inch closer to John too, and though some mocked Langa behind his back, they stopped when they realized Shaka himself seemed pleased.

Then, one morning, the king called for John directly.

He was escorted to the great fire circle, where Shaka sat alone, a thick leopard skin across his shoulders, his hair bound in tight braids. The interpreter stood beside him, silent until summoned.

John knelt.

Shaka spoke. The interpreter translated.

"You left your home not for war, but for love. For your mother."

"Yes," John said, his voice steady.

"She must be strong, this mother of yours, to raise a boy who walks like a man."

John swallowed. "She was strong. But she was sick when I left. I came to find a way to help her."

The interpreter relayed the words.

Shaka did not speak at first. He stared at John with eyes like polished obsidian, then finally said something that the interpreter stumbled over when translating.

"He says there is power in such love. More than in any spear."

A pause. Then Shaka nodded once, and John was dismissed.

That night, Langa brought him a string of beads woven with colors John had not seen before—deep blues and ochres, the kind worn only by those with status.

"What is this?" John asked.

Langa touched his own chest, then John's.

"Brother," he said softly.

John sat very still.

He had come to Africa a boy without a compass, carrying only guilt and hope. Somehow, in the heart of a warrior's kraal, among the spears and ghosts, he had found not only survival—but respect.

And in Langa, he had found something else. A bridge.

Something was changing. And soon, John knew, the world would begin to shift beneath his feet again.

The rains came at last. They rolled over the high veldt like drums from the sky, pounding the thatched huts, soaking the red soil to black. The days grew misty and green. Mornings were slower now, with smoke rising from cookfires and the children running half-naked through the puddles. John no longer flinched when the spears clattered or the warriors roared. He had, in his own strange way, become part of the place.

Still, he ached.

His mother's name lived behind his ribs like a stone. He dreamed of her often now—sometimes frail, sometimes strong, always waiting. He knew it could not last. This pause in the storm, this strange season of grace inside Shaka's kraal—it was borrowed time.

One morning, he was summoned again.

This time there were no warriors in the circle. Only Shaka, seated beneath the carved post of his ceremonial shelter, and Langa. The interpreter stood beside the king with a solemn face.

John bowed, then waited.

The interpreter began slowly. "Shaka says... the sun rises even when we do not ask it to. He says your time in the kraal has been full of light."

John blinked. "I don't understand."

"You are to be sent home."

The words dropped like thunder.

"Home?" John echoed. "But I—how?"

Shaka raised a hand and spoke, voice calm and low.

"He says," the interpreter continued, "that warriors who walk through fire for love must not be kept in cages. He says you may return to your mother. And that you will not go alone."

From behind the hut, a line of men appeared—thirty warriors in full regalia, shields and assegais in hand, their heads high. And behind them—Farewell and Fynn, newly dressed and standing tall despite their gauntness. William, too, stepped forward with wide, blinking eyes, as though he'd just been shaken awake from a long dream.

John couldn't move.

"He is giving you safe escort to Delagoa Bay," said the interpreter. "No harm shall touch you before the ocean's edge."

John's throat burned. "And my—my mother?"

Shaka murmured a few words, then gestured to a young boy carrying a cloth-wrapped parcel.

The interpreter explained: "This is ivory. The finest from the royal stores. You will sell it there—for many coins. He says... that will be your spear."

Shaka says something else, and then hands John some European coins likely taken from previous encounters.

The interpreter says, "Shaka also gives you these coins from people of other lands, which may be useful to you. They are not useful to Shaka.

John took the bundle and the coins with shaking hands.

"Tell the king," John said slowly, "I will never forget this. I will never forget him."

Shaka nodded and spoke again. The interpreter delivered his words in English to John: "The king also wants you to know that Langa has requested permission to travel with you to Delgoa Bay. The great king has granted him permission."

Langa suddenly broke into a wide grin, and John wanted to rush forward and embrace his new friend but Zulu etiquette kept his feet rooted to the dirt floor.

Then, to John's surprise, he rose from his seat. The great king walked toward him with slow, deliberate steps. When he reached John, he looked down, studied the red hair, the sun-cracked skin, the callused feet. Then he touched John's shoulder and spoke without an interpreter.

"You walk far," Shaka said, his accent thick but the words clear. "But love walk farther."

Then he turned and disappeared into the kraal, his shadow falling long behind him. It was the last time John would ever see him.

CHAPTER 29

The morning of their departure from the kraal came with little fanfare. The sky was pale and high, streaked with chalk-colored wisps, and the air carried the faint smell of dung fires. John stood by the palisade fence with Langa beside him—barefoot, alert-eyed, and grinning faintly.

The farewell was quiet. Langa stood at the edge of the outer gate, arms folded. He did not speak, but he did nod—once, slowly—before slipping back into the reeds.

John stared after him, heart knotted.

Then he turned to William, Farewell, and Fynn, who were lining up behind the Zulu escort, still dazed by their sudden deliverance.

Among the colorful entourage was a wiry older man named Mabaso, wrapped in a woven red shawl over one shoulder and wearing a necklace of brass rings. Mabaso was introduced to John with a formal nod. He was Shaka's appointed interpreter for the escort—fluent in Zulu, isiXhosa, and passable English, having once lived among Portuguese traders near Lourenço Marques. His role was clear—he would ensure John's words reached others accurately, and more importantly, speak for Shaka if needed once they arrived in Delagoa Bay.

As the party moved through the tall grass, John looked over his shoulder at the kraal that had once held him prisoner and later kept him safe.

The sky was wide, the path ahead long. But this time, he would not walk it alone. And this time, he carried more than hope—he carried a gift from a king.

Langa walked with quiet energy. Though most of the warriors gave the favored boy a wide berth, it was clear he had chosen his place—right beside John. Their bond had become known, even to Shaka. And while Langa had picked up some English phrases—most of them fragments learned by ear—he spoke them only when Mabaso was out of earshot, as if their halting exchange was a private game between them.

"You ready?" Langa asked, eyes bright.

John nodded, hoisting his satchel. "More than ready."

"You... go see big water," Langa said, tapping his chest. "I go too."

John smiled. "Yes. Together."

The group moved out at a steady pace, drumming feet against the dirt. John had worn the same softened hide tunic since his arrival in the kraal, and now with a carved walking stick and a short-sword gifted by one of the warriors, he looked more like a barefoot scout than a runaway Scottish boy.

As they descended through thick ridges and into sunlit bushveld, Mabaso walked near the front, exchanging occasional words with their lead warrior. John and Langa walked together, side by side, while the rest fanned out in a loose diamond around them.

By mid-morning, the sun had risen high enough to bake the earth beneath their feet, and Langa glanced at John's flushed face.

"You red," he said. "Hot boy."

John laughed. "Red hair. Red face. No escape."

Langa didn't get the joke, but he grinned anyway.

Mabaso turned his head slightly. "The boy is teasing you," he said dryly. "Better keep your wits."

"I've come this far," John replied. "I'm not losing them now."

They camped that night beside a narrow river, and the men built fires in a ring. Langa sat beside John, skin glowing amber in the firelight, hands cupped around a bowl of roasted roots. Mabaso translated occasionally when the warriors told stories—tales of past battles, lion hunts, even a man who survived a crocodile bite by stabbing it in the eye.

But John's attention was drawn upward, to the stars. He hadn't realized until that moment how close they might be to Delagoa Bay. Just a few more days, perhaps. And then—what?

He rubbed the soles of his feet, hardened like horn after months of barefoot travel, and watched the sparks rise. Langa glanced at him, then offered a second root.

"You think much," the boy said.

"I have a lot to think about."

Langa nodded, then pointed upward. "Star move. We move too."

"Yes," John said softly. "Almost there."

And somewhere, not so far beyond the river, the ocean waited.

The jungle gave way to a stretch of hilly woodland by the time they made camp on the third evening. The forest still breathed with insects and leaf-hiss, but now, in the spaces between trees, John caught glimpses of lower valleys—of land sloping toward some unseen basin. The air had changed, too. It felt heavier. Damp and scented with salt.

He walked close to Langa as they descended a narrow track. The youth was quieter than usual, spear strapped across his back, eyes flicking from tree to tree. Late in the morning, they crested a low ridge and saw below them a scatter of huts—round, thatched, and arranged in no clear pattern. A thin wisp of smoke curled upward. A small village. Not Zulu.

One of the younger warriors barked a command, and the whole escort paused.

"They want to raid it," Mabaso said bluntly, glancing back. "Not Zulu. Not under Shaka. They think it's a weak place."

John stepped forward. "No. That village hasn't done anything. There are children down there."

The warriors ignored him. A few were already descending.

John looked to Mabaso. "Tell them Shaka would not want this."

Mabaso gave an almost amused snort. "They won't believe that."

John turned to Langa. "Say something. Please."

Langa looked torn. His jaw tightened. But then he stepped up to the nearest warrior, one of the more respected elders of the party, and held out a flat hand.

"Shaka gave us a task," Langa said in slow, careful Zulu. "To bring this boy to the sea. With honor. With pride. Not with fire."

There was a pause. Several warriors muttered.

"He is our friend," Langa went on, raising his chin. "He earned the shield of Shaka. He must go home to save his mother."

A quiet settled over the ridge. The elder warrior studied Langa, then looked at John, his eyes lingering on the matted red hair, the darkened skin, the callused bare feet.

With a snort, he turned back to the others and spat into the dirt. "We don't waste time on rats," he said in Zulu, and began walking again, away from the village.

One by one, the others followed.

Langa exhaled slowly. John nodded at him with something between gratitude and disbelief. "You did that."

Langa shrugged. "Shaka say you not be harmed."

"That's not the same as saving a village."

"It is today."

They walked on.

That night, they built a low fire and kept it small. The warriors seemed more subdued. Perhaps they also felt the ocean's breath rising inland. Or perhaps the weight of the Langas protest lingered in ways none could name. No one spoke of the village again.

John lay awake for some time, listening to the crackling branches and the wind that whispered through wet leaves. He thought of his mother. Of the *Mary*. Of Farewell and Fynn and the long braid of decisions that had led him to this moment.

At last, sleep took him.

The next morning, the jungle thinned out. Ferns gave way to sandy brush, and the air tasted unmistakably of the sea.

Langa walked beside John, quiet but alert, his spear resting across his shoulders.

The translator turned toward John and grunted. "Another day or two," he muttered. "Then the sea."

The jungle deepened with silence as the sun edged downward, casting long, gold-tinted spears of light through the trees. John had grown used to the soft thump of bare Zulu feet behind him, the snatches of quiet talk, the rustle of assegais brushing thorny undergrowth. Langa walked near him, ever alert, ever smiling in that tight-lipped way of his that hinted more thoughts than he said aloud.

They had been traveling since dawn with only one short rest. John was beginning to anticipate nearing the coast—he could smell salt in the air now, and the jungle was thinning even more. Hope had stirred in his chest all day like a bird that wouldn't quiet.

Then it happened. A sharp hiss—a blur in the underbrush—and a cry of pain. One of the warriors staggered back, dropping his shield. Blood flowed from two quick punctures on his ankle. The man's name was Mvelase, and the others leaped into motion as he fell.

"Snake," Mabaso said quickly. Langa knelt, eyes wide. Another man sliced open the bite with a small knife and pressed the flesh in rhythmic pulses, trying to force the venom out.

"What kind of snake?" John asked, moving toward them.

Mabaso replied quietly, "Night adder, maybe. Or worse."

Mvelase's eyes revealed his pain and fear.

"We have to move," John said. "Delagoa Bay will have someone... someone who can help him."

The warriors looked doubtful. One said something to Langa in a low voice. Langa answered curtly and turned back to John.

"They say he is a warrior. If death comes, he will not shame himself."

"No," John said, rising to his full height. "He came all this way to protect me. I won't let him die in the dust if I can help it."

Langa clearly didn't understand all the English words, but understood the import of them.

The group rearranged themselves. Mvelase was lifted onto a makeshift litter of two shields and some lashed spears. The pace became urgent now. John could feel his own heartbeat pounding with each step. The thought of being so close—so very close—and losing someone to a stupid, hidden snake twisted inside him.

They reached the jungle's edge just as the sun reached the horizon. The air changed. Palm fronds swayed above the mangroves. White smoke from cookfires curled on the breeze. And there, beyond the tide line, were the low roofs of Delagoa Bay.

"Keep your spears down," John said, stepping forward.

But it didn't matter. As they appeared from the foliage—thirty Zulu warriors and one pale, red-haired boy—shouts rang out. Two Portuguese traders dropped their barrels and ran. A woman shrieked and bolted into her house. A rifle was raised from a rooftop.

John walked slowly, palms raised, his voice loud and clear.

"Don't shoot! I'm one of you! I'm here with friends!"

No one moved. Langa stepped forward beside him, placing a hand on John's shoulder. The gesture was confusing to the townsfolk but oddly calming.

Then one of the villagers—an older woman with dark eyes and a kerchief tight around her chin—squinted hard at John.

"That boy," she whispered. "The one with red hair."

A murmur swept through the gathering crowd. "Impossible," he said. "A white boy leading a band of Zulus!"

Mvelase groaned loudly on the litter behind John.

"Please," John shouted. "He's been bitten by a snake. Is there a doctor here?"

A woman nodded and pointed toward the far end of the port. "Go to Dr. Costa. He's treated worse."

John exhaled. He turned to Langa and the warriors and gave a nod. "Let's move."

And so the boy and his escort of Zulu fighters, half-silhouetted against the red spill of early evening, entered Delagoa Bay, and a legend was born of a white boy leading a peaceful band of Zulus into a port town in Africa.

CHAPTER 30

The doctor's house was little more than a two-room structure of whitewashed stone and timber, its shutters half-hinged and a single lamp burning in the window. Inside, it smelled of camphor and boiled linen. A young assistant—likely more porter than nurse—helped the snake-bitten warrior onto a makeshift cot while John, still half-reeling from the journey, tried to explain what had happened. The man's leg was already swelling.

"I don't know what kind of snake it was," John said, "but he cried out before we even saw it. One of the others said it was *imfezi*—a puff adder."

The doctor—a wiry Portuguese man named Eusebio Costa—examined the wound by lamplight. His hands were steady, his tone clinical. "If it was *imfezi*, we'll be lucky to keep his leg, or his life. But you brought him quickly. That counts for something."

Something in Costa's demeanor told John the man didn't like helping the warrior.

"You don't want to help a Zulu?" John asked.

"Seems odd, is all. Spent years fearing them. And for free?"

John found the coins that Shaka had given him as a parting gift and handed them to Costa. "Is this enough?"

Costa's eyes beamed. He knew they were worth much more than enough.

He began cleaning the wound with more vigor, then ordered his assistant to fetch several jars from the shelf.

John stood aside, watching as the warrior grimaced, sweat running down his temples. Langa hovered nearby, arms crossed but face stricken, as if the man's pain were his own. The others remained outside, a silent perimeter of spears in the dusk.

"Does he speak any English?" the doctor asked.

"No," John said. "But he came here to protect me."

The doctor gave a low hum of approval. "I'll do what I can."

He worked methodically—opening the wound, applying a poultice of crushed leaves soaked in clear alcohol, wrapping it with strips of linen—and for a while there was no sound but the utterances of pain and the grumbling of Zulu warriors in the shadows outside.

Then the doctor leaned back, squinting past the lamplight to study John's face more carefully.

"You're not Portuguese," he said.

"No," John replied. "Scottish."

The doctor's eyes narrowed further. "Scottish. Red hair. About twelve or so?"

"Thirteen now."

"Wait here." The doctor rose, went into the adjoining room, and returned with a rough leather ledger in one hand. He flipped through several pages, then stopped. "About a month ago, there was a man here. Scottish. Crippled. Missing an arm and a leg. I treated him for an abscess at the base of his wooden limb. Told me he was looking for his son."

John's breath hitched. "Did he have a name?"

"I don't remember him saying. But he said his son had red hair. Like yours."

John could barely speak. "He was here?"

The doctor nodded, frowning slightly. "He waited in this godforsaken town for weeks. Stubborn, hopeful man. Then, three days ago, he came back to see me. Seemed broken by his waiting. Said he'd accepted you were gone and signed on with a Dutch vessel heading back toward the Cape. Odd timing, but it left today, not long ago."

John rushed to the door and looked out toward the water. The sea was bathed in the orange and plum shadows of twilight, but far on the horizon, a single sail was visible—shrinking slowly into the night.

He gripped the doorway, his voice barely a whisper. "That was my father…"

Behind him, Langa stepped forward, puzzled. "On the ship?"

John nodded. For a moment, there was silence in the doorway except for the distant cries of seabirds and the hush of waves brushing the sand.

Then the doctor appeared beside him, placing a hand on his shoulder. "I'm sorry," he said quietly. "He waited longer than most men would in this place."

John felt the ache of it settle deep in his chest. He had crossed a continent. Survived hyenas and hippos and war. He had befriended a king and carried hope like fire through rain. And now, after all that, the man he came to find was vanishing into the horizon.

"Might come back," Langa said, as if searching John's face for a trace of certainty.

But John could not answer. He only stood in the doorway, watching the final curve of sail dissolve into the darkening sea.

The sky over Delagoa Bay had turned to charcoal streaked with purple and cloud-smothered stars. Within the small house of Dr. Costa, the snake-bitten warrior slept—his leg elevated, wrapped in a salve-soaked cloth, and watched closely by two of his companions, who refused to leave his side. Outside, the Zulu escort had formed a silent camp beneath the moonless canopy, their fire low and their expressions inscrutable.

John had not spoken for some time.

He sat on a wooden bench beside the open window, elbows on his knees, staring down at his feet covered with mud from three kingdoms. But his mind was far out at sea, chasing a ship he could no longer see.

Langa sat across from him, holding a piece of dry bread between his fingers, turning it over thoughtfully. He had not touched it. He had barely moved since sundown.

"Mvelase might have died," Langa said quietly, nodding toward the inner room.

"I know."

"You saved him."

"I just brought him here," John replied.

Langa gave a small shake of the head and spoke in his native tongue. The ever-present Mabaso interpreted. "He said Mvelase would have died out there. You carried him when the others grew tired. You argued for him when the white people feared him. You don't see what you are. But I do."

John looked up at him. "I don't feel like anything."

Langa's voice lowered. "You feel... like son... who lost his father."

The silence that followed hung thick. John opened his mouth once, closed it, then tried again.

Then, through Mabaso, John and Langa more easily spoke. "He was here, Langa," John said. "I was so close. If we hadn't stopped at that village... if the snake hadn't bitten Mvelase..."

"A whole village was spared because of you," Langa said simply.

John blinked.

"You lost one man," Langa continued. "You might have lost another—Mvelase—if we had not stopped to bleed him and breought him to the medicine man. He was a warrior. One whc protected you." He paused. "Would your father be proud if you had let a man die just so you could see him?"

John exhaled slowly. "I don't know."

"I think not," Langa said. "If he is the kind of man who came across the sea to find his son, then he is the kind of man who would want that son to carry others, too."

John leaned back against the cool stone wall and let those interpreted words settle. For the first time, something inside him eased.

A few minutes later, Dr. Costa emerged from the back room, wiping his hands on a towel. "He's resting. The swelling's still bad, but I think we've slowed the poison. He'll need days. Maybe weeks. But he has a chance now."

John stood. "Thank you."

Costa nodded. "It wasn't just me. He wouldn't be alive if you hadn't brought him."

"Still… thank you."

Costa eyed John a little longer, then added, "There's something else. I remembered something your father said before he left."

John's breath caught again.

"He said, 'Tell the boy, if he ever comes—tell him I forgive him for leaving. Tell him his mother would have been proud of him.'"

John lowered his head. His hands clenched at his sides.

"I didn't know what it meant at the time," the doctor added, "but now I suppose I do."

John nodded. His voice was almost raw. "So do I." For the first time, John knew in his heart that his mother had died… or his father would not have come to Africa. So, he was mourning two losses.

Behind him, Langa watched carefully.

When John turned to face him, the trace of sorrow was still there—but also something steadier.

"What do we do now?" Langa asked.

John looked around the small room—the cot, the shuttered windows, the flicker of firelight beyond. "We stay," he said. "Until Mvelase can walk again."

"And after?"

John's eyes lifted toward the dark beyond the bay. Through Mabaso he said, "I find a ship. A safe one. I go back and rescue my mates from the *Mary*. I didn't survive all this just to forget them."

Langa gave a faint, amused nod. "Then I go with you."

They sat in quiet understanding, two boys on the edge of something larger than either had imagined. Behind them, Mvelase stirred and coughed once in his sleep, and somewhere far out on the horizon, the wind shifted faintly against a sail.

The sea was silver the next morning. Gulls floated on the breeze and dipped toward the waves, and a thin, cool mist hovered where water met land. John Ross walked alone along the stony edge of Delagoa Bay, his bare feet pressing cold into the sand, his arms drawn across his chest. The boy who had crossed a continent now walked like an old man—slow, uncertain, hollow with longing.

A high ledge jutted to his right, not far above the waterline, and he climbed it without thinking, drawn to its quiet elevation. From the top, he could see the horizon in all directions, the early sun glinting off the ocean like a field of shattered glass.

It was too much.

He had come all this way. He had survived the *Mary*, the hyenas, the hippos, the battle, the kraal. But he had lost his father.

A low cry from above pulled his gaze skyward. A bird—large, dark, familiar—circled overhead. Its wings stretched wide and solemn as it passed over him, angling toward the sea.

He had seen one just like it the day he had shot a hare on the cliffs of Scotland. The day he decided he would have to leave his father and mother behind.

His throat ached, and his hands clenched at his sides. It was all for nothing. His mother gone. His father lost. The flame of purpose that had carried him across an entire continent now flickered against the chill of loneliness.

And then—

A figure appeared.

Down below. Along the strand where the tide whispered across the sand, a man walked with a hard, lurching gait. One leg stiff and wooden. One sleeve pinned to his side. Bent against the wind like a stump that would not fall.

John froze.

He could not breathe. Could not speak. Could only stare.

The man turned slightly, glancing toward the bluff as he limped closer to the water's edge.

His hair was longer than John remembered. His face gaunter. But the shape was unmistakable. The jaw. The stubborn tilt of the head.

"Da?" John whispered.

The man paused mid-step.

John stepped forward. "Da!" he called out.

The man looked up, blinked. His eyes squinted against the sun.

John was already running—down the slope, over the rocks, toward the shore.

Lewis Ross took a halting step forward. "John?"

And then the boy was there—throwing his arms around the man, burying his face in the rough, briny fabric of his coat.

Lewis dropped to his knees, as much from shock as from the sudden embrace, and wrapped his single arm around the trembling boy.

They said nothing for a long time.

When Lewis finally pulled back, he cupped John's face in a callused hand. "I stayed," he said simply. "I just couldn't leave. I thought… if you were still alive, you'd come here."

"I did," John said, laughing through his tears. "I came as fast as I could."

Lewis nodded, eyes red. "I'll never let you go again, son. Never."

Above them, the wind picked up. The great bird circled once more, then turned inland, fading into the morning light.

EPILOGUE

The rescue of the *Mary* crew came less than three weeks after John and Lewis were reunited. With Nathaniel Isaacs's uncle arranging the funding and a Portuguese vessel hired from Delagoa Bay, they set out upriver with supplies and medicine. The survivors were found, weak but alive, and wept openly when they saw John and Lewis on the ship's deck.

Lieutenant Farewell and Dr. Fynn eventually returned to Cape Town. Whatever dreams they once had of taming the interior of the continent had vanished. Neither man would speak again of what happened in the kraal of the Zulu king.

William, ever adaptable, shipped out again not long after. He served aboard several vessels along the African coast, always looking for steady work and keeping one ear turned toward tales of red-haired boys and jungle kings.

As for Langa, the boy who once belonged to the silence of Shaka's shadow, he returned to the royal kraal with honor. What became of him after that remains unknown. Some say he rose to command warriors. Others whisper he was seen, years later, far from the kingdom, wearing English boots and carrying an ivory-handled blade.

Mvelase, the snake-bitten Zulu warrior, recovered after three weeks without losing a limb. He and Dr. Costa became friendly, and Mvelase eventually became an assistant to Dr. Costa and was influential in protecting Delagoa Bay from Zulu attacks.

Nathaniel Isaacs, at seventeen, pressed farther into the interior. He became one of the youngest European explorers of his age, writing extensively about the people he met and the kingdoms he briefly touched. Some criticized his accounts. Others called them visionary. But no one questioned that his feet had walked where few dared to tread.

And John Ross? He stayed by his father's side. For a time. Some said they returned together to Scotland. Others believe they ventured again into the interior. There were whispers of a red-haired young man who could speak Zulu like a native and walk barefoot across thorned trails without flinching. But stories twist over time. Only this is certain—father and son had found each other again.

Margaret's Letter to Lewis

My dearest Lewis,

If you're reading this, then perhaps there's still a road left for you. Or a sail. Or a wind. I pray that's true.

I don't have many words left in me. Each breath now feels like it's borrowed, and I am tired in a way that can't be slept off. But before I go, I need to write you this—not to haunt you, but to leave behind something gentle. Something you might carry without shame.

You were not always kind, Lewis. Not to me. And not to yourself. But I know you loved us. Even in the silence. Even in the drink. I saw it in the way you watched John sleep when he was small, and in the way you would sit outside the door after an argument, too proud to knock but too guilty to walk away.

There was good in you. Still is. And I believe there's more ahead for you than regret.

I don't know where John has gone. Maybe he's chasing the dream you once had and forgot. Or maybe he's just trying to outrun your shadow. But if you ever find him, Lewis—if—please tell him that I never stopped loving him. Not for one breath. Not for one heartbeat. And that I forgave you both before either of you asked.

This world is full of cruel reckonings. Don't let this be one of them.

Find our boy, if you can. Come home together, if God allows. And if not—then at least let John know what it means to keep going.

With love that never wore out,

Margaret

ABOUT THE
SOURCE MATERIAL

In the late 1970s, I was a filmmaker in Minnesota and founder of a motion picture production company looking to begin producing entertainment films. One day, two producers from South Africa showed up at our studio with a proposal for us to co-produce a 10-part television series entitled SHAKA THE WARRIOR KING. They gave us a packet of materials describing the research and storyline, and while we did not have the funds to invest, I was smitten by a single paragraph in the synopsis about a boy named John Ross who in 1820 became shipwrecked on the Natal Coast of Africa and had to trek nearly 400 miles across the mostly unexplored continent to find rescue. Along the way, he encountered the mighty Zulu nation and its fierce king, Shaka, surviving to tell the tale.

Not much more was known about John Ross, but later, in the Library of Congress, I found a republished traveler's journal written by a contemporary of John Ross named Nathaniel Isaacs who was also on the ship that floundered at sea. This two-volume journal contained more information about John Ross and the Zulus. But it lacked any background information about the boy, which allowed me to fill in the blanks. The result is this novel, which I hope you will enjoy.